# THE HERNE'S EGG

# IRISH DRAMATIC TEXTS

GENERAL EDITOR
Robert Mahony
The Catholic University of America

EDITORIAL BOARD
Bernard Benstock
University of Miami

David R. Clark
University of Massachusetts

Philip Edwards
University of Liverpool

Maurice Harmon
University College, Dublin

Shirley Strum Kenny
Queens College
The City University of New York

Ann Saddlemyer
University of Toronto

# THE HERNE'S EGG

by W. B. Yeats

Edited
with an Introduction and Notes
by Andrew Parkin

The Catholic University of America Press
Washington, D.C.

Colin Smythe
Gerrards Cross, Bucks.

Copyright © 1938 by William Butler Yeats
Copyright renewed 1966 by Mrs. Georgie Yeats,
Michael B. Yeats, and Miss Anne Yeats

This edition is reprinted by arrangement with Macmillan
Publishing Company, a division of Macmillan, Inc.

Introduction and other editorial matter copyright © 1991
The Catholic University of America Press
Printed in the United States of America

The paper used in this publication meets the minimum
requirements of American National Standards for
Information Science—Permanence of Paper for Printed
Library materials, ANSI Z39.48-1984.
∞

LIBRARY OF CONGRESS CATALOGING-IN-PUBLICATION DATA
Yeats, W. B. (William Butler), 1865–1939.
 The Herne's egg / by W. B. Yeats ; edited with an
introduction and notes by Andrew Parkin.
  p. cm. — (Irish dramatic texts)
 Includes bibliographical references.
 ISBN 0-8132-0742-8
 I. Parkin, Andrew, 1937– . II. Title. III. Series.
PR5904.H4 1991
822'.8—dc20          90-24235

BRITISH LIBRARY CATALOGUING IN PUBLICATION DATA
Yeats, W. B. (William Butler, 1865–1939)
 The herne's egg.
  1. English drama
  I. Parkin, Andrew, 1937–
  822.8
  ISBN 0-86140-343-6

# CONTENTS

Acknowledgments  vi

Abbreviations  viii

Preface  ix

Introduction  1

Note on the Text  33

Critical Bibliography  36

*The Herne's Egg*  39

ACKNOWLEDGMENTS

My research for this edition of *The Herne's Egg* was supported by a grant from the Social Sciences and Humanities Research Council of Canada; I am grateful also to the University of British Columbia for having given me a sabbatical leave in order to work on the play. Individual scholars have helped me by their previous work on Yeats, debts which I record in notes and the bibliography. My thanks of a more personal kind should not go unexpressed: Michael Sidnell gave me good advice and encouragement; David Clarke genially agreed that I should proceed with the edition; anonymous scholars of the Canadian Federation for the Humanities gave very careful advice, much of which I have used to advantage; Sidney Poger discussed with me his student production of the play at the University of Vermont and lent me a tape recording of that accomplished production; Mary O'Malley gave me her time, hospitality, and helpful copies of material relating to her successful professional production at the Lyric Theatre, Belfast; Jim Flannery's exciting production and his writing on Yeats in general were confirmations of my own assessment of the play's stageworthiness; students of dance and drama with whom I worked on a studio production of the play helped me to discover its vivid theatrical force as well as the confusions in the text revealed by this edition; my greatest scholarly debt, though, is to Alison Armstrong, who generously gave me a copy of her transcription and edition of the manuscript version of the play prepared for the Cornell Yeats Manuscript Series.

When I studied the manuscript in the National Library of Ireland, the staff were as ever prompt to help and friendly. I am grateful too for Ms. Cathy Henderson's similarly courteous efficiency at the Harry Ransom Humanities Research Center, the University of Texas at Austin, where I studied the typescript of the play.

I gratefully acknowledge permission to use the textual ma-

## ACKNOWLEDGMENTS

terial and to quote from other works by Yeats given by Anne and Michael Yeats, A. P. Watt, and Macmillan of London.

Finally, for their careful work typing and retyping the editorial material, I am grateful to Mme. Françoise Lentsch, Mrs. Debbie Onbirbak, and Mrs. Toby Mayes. Errors and weaknesses in the edition are solely my responsibility.

# ABBREVIATIONS

| | |
|---|---|
| Com. Pl. | A. N. Jeffares and A. S. Knowland, *A Commentary on the Collected Plays of W. B. Yeats* (Stanford: Stanford Univ. Press, 1975) |
| Congal | Sir Samuel Ferguson, *Congal, A Poem in Five Books* (Dublin: Ponsonby, 1872) |
| E & I | *Essays and Introductions* (London: Macmillan, 1961) |
| Geeta | *The Geeta*, trans. Shri Purohit Swami (London: Faber and Faber, 1935) |
| Oxford Book | *The Oxford Book of Modern Verse, 1892–1935*, ed. W. B. Yeats (London: Oxford Univ. Press, 1966) |
| Scribner's TS | Typescript of *The Herne's Egg*, Humanities Research Center, Univ. of Texas, Austin |
| Variorum | *The Variorum Edition of the Plays of W. B. Yeats*, ed. Russell K. Alspach (London: Macmillan/New York: Macmillan, 1966) |
| Vision | W. B. Yeats, *A Vision* (New York: Macmillan, 1961) |
| Wade | *The Letters of W. B. Yeats*, ed. Allan Wade (London: Hart-Davies, 1954; New York: Macmillan, 1966) |
| WMA | G. Melchiori, *The Whole Mystery of Art* (London: Routledge & Kegan Paul, 1960) |
| Y and T | F. A. C. Wilson, *W. B. Yeats and Tradition* (London: Gollancz, 1961) |
| YTCH | *W. B. Yeats: The Critical Heritage*, ed. A. N. Jeffares (London: Routledge & Kegan Paul, 1977) |
| 1952 | W. B. Yeats, *Collected Plays* (London: Macmillan, 1952) |
| 1938 | W. B. Yeats, *The Herne's Egg* (London: Macmillan, 1938) |

# PREFACE

For the most mordant satirist, there are moments when all offend. This includes the satirist himself; none shall 'scape whipping. Yeats's last three plays, *The Herne's Egg* (1938), *Purgatory* (1939) and *The Death of Cuchulain* (1939) are differing expressions of this state of mind. *The Herne's Egg* is the lightest of the three in mood and tone. "Herne" is an archaic and dialect version of heron. In *Calvary* (1920) Yeats had used the modern spelling but altered "heron" to "herne" in MS8770 of *The Herne's Egg*. The dialect version fits better the Irish setting and unfamiliarity of the play's action, though the bird is a symbol in both plays of lonely, subjective deity. Despite its bloodshed, murder, rape, and suicide, Yeats still finds in *The Herne's Egg* farcical humor lit by a smiling comic moon. In short, his treatment of Congal's story is deliberately ambivalent. This no doubt suited its place in his canon as a last backward glance to the comedy of *The Player Queen* (1922) before the darkness of his final two plays. His *selbst-ironie* comes out in the profanity and violence of the action, the relative exuberance of staging that abandons the austerity of his earlier dance plays, and the comic treatment of his characteristic symbols. In *The Player Queen* Yeats had envisaged the herald of each new great cycle of history as an Old Beggar whose back itches so as to set him rolling in straw and braying like a donkey, as if he were a reincarnation of "the donkey that carried Christ into Jerusalem" (*Variorum* 254). The image is reversed in *The Herne's Egg*, where an old Clare highwayman has been reincarnated and brought on stage as a life-size toy donkey which brays after Congal's death. The presence of this jocular stage property directly affects the mood of any scene in which it appears. It suggests what in *The Player Queen* the Old Beggar tells Decima: the only thing he has known ever to come from the land of the dead is "an old jackass" (*Variorum* 754). Similarly at the end of *The Herne's Egg*, we are left with nothing to show for all the struggle of man and bird—

## PREFACE

god but "just another donkey." In his satirical "irresponsibility" Yeats seems to be laughing at any attempt to reaffirm his old heroic values, and at the same time suggesting that the donkey, humble creature as it is, yet symbolizes the triumph of the Christ-God who was carried by it through the streets of Jerusalem. But if a man may be reborn as an animal, a nature god may be replaced by a man-god. *The Herne's Egg* demonstrates the brilliant way in which Yeats could use a long narrative source such as *Congal* (1872) and make of it a short play full of strange effects, experimental and absurdist, years before that strain of modern theater became well known or provided dramatists with a powerful antirealistic style. The play is also remarkable for its development of a new dramatic verse capable of great flexibility for dialogue and which Yeats used with supreme skill in his next play, *Purgatory*. *The Herne's Egg* is, then, remarkable for a number of reasons. Nor should we forget that it is the fullest dramatic expression of Yeats's interest in Indian thought. Yet there is no "orientalism," no pursuit of the exotic for its own sake, no use of fake "Indian" settings or local color.

The unsavory subject of gang rape ensured that some contemporary reviewers, especially in Ireland, condemned the play. In fact, Yeats's stage action is never tasteless or merely sensational. The play deserves recognition as an exuberant and crucial landmark in Yeatsian drama. But it is one of the most difficult and mysterious of his texts. For these reasons, there is a real need for an annotated edition of *The Herne's Egg*.

# INTRODUCTION

## BACKGROUND

*The Herne's Egg* relates to earlier works in Yeats's canon in a number of ways. Its combination of the heroic with the farcical aligns it with *The Green Helmet* (1910). It is linked to *A Vision* (1925) and *The Player Queen* through its concern with turbulent events presaging a reversal of opposing historical cones.

In *A Vision* Yeats presents a view of human life and history that shows all creation as having fragmented into opposing antinomies, the only perfect unity being imagined as a phaseless sphere which cannot be understood and appears distorted from a human point of view, so that the sphere seems to be a cone. This divine sphere is called the thirteenth cone. The differing types of human beings are symbolized by twenty-six lunar phases. The remaining phases, numbers one (the totally eclipsed moon) and fifteen (the perfect full moon), belong to supernatural beings only. The phases clustering around phase one, total objectivity, are objective phases characterized by self-sacrifice, subservience, and group behavior. Those clustering around phase fifteen, total subjectivity, are subjective, characterized by the pursuit of the self, lonely distinction, subjective beauty. These objective and subjective phases Yeats also imagines as two historical principles he calls cones or gyres; such eras are inaugurated by the birth of a god whose power over human history and people waxes until at the widest point of a historical gyre an opposing god is born, the gyre or cone or age reverses itself and a new age develops until another reversal of the gyres. Thus the subjective pagan age inaugurated by Dionysus gives way to an objective age inaugurated by Christ. The god is born as a result of a mystic marriage between a god and a woman. *The Herne's Egg* is one of the plays written after Yeats had worked out this elaborate symbolic view of reality: its action depicts the violence at a reversal of historical gyres or cones; and its characterization includes three significant figures from *A Vision*'s schema of lunar phases: the hunchback, saint, and fool assigned respectively to phases twenty-six, twenty-seven, and twenty-eight.

As with *The Player Queen,* there is a donkey that heralds the reversal of gyres, and a mixture of seriousness and humor in the play. But *The Herne's Egg* is also like *The Resurrection* (1931), *The King of the Great Clock Tower* (1935), and *A Full Moon in March* (1935), for all were variants of the dance-play pattern Yeats established in *Four Plays for Dancers* (1921), written under the influence of Japanese Noh drama. The post-Noh group, while still retaining such conventions as the dancer directed by supernatural energies, was written for public stage rather than private drawing room. *The Herne's Egg* pursues the themes of icy virgin and profane lover, "desecration and the lover's night," and the death of the hero, explored in *A Full Moon in March.* It also, in my view, extends the Christian theme of *Calvary* (1920) and *The Resurrection,* sharing with *Calvary* the image of the heron as a symbol of antithetical, subjective deity and echoing the theme of *The Resurrection,* the changeover from a pagan to a Christian era. In a sense it is a play that takes stock of the last half of Yeats's dramatic work, rather as his poem "The Circus Animals' Desertion" takes stock of his career as poet and playwright together. In making gang rape central to its action, Yeats conforms to the "mound of refuse" theory of his creative impulse to be found in "The Circus Animals' Desertion" and explores the mysterious profanity of the sacred marriage of virgin and god which was the theme also for "Leda and the Swan" and "A Stick of Incense." The sacred marriage of the mortal Attracta to the herne god, consummated through the rape by Congal and his men, is an image of the soul's links with eternity above and "the fury and the mire of human veins" below.

By constructing a plot the events of which can be interpreted at once on a spiritual and an all-too-human level, Yeats brings together in merciless self-parody and satire both sides of his poetical character. The youthful poet who became a spiritual quester, seeker of arcane spiritual knowledge, cohabits in the play with the older, earthy Yeats pursuing the sensual side of his nature and imagination through such personae as Crazy Jane and the wild, wicked old man of *On the Boiler* (1939). While the play expresses the Indian philosophy of his friend of the mid-1930s, Shri Purohit Swami, its use of reincarnation goes back to the very young Yeats, who encountered Mohini Chatterjee's Indian thought. The play's

INTRODUCTION

prime source in Sir Samuel Ferguson's poem *Congal* reminds us that Yeats explored his Irish background from very early in his career. And even on the level of detail, the battles perfectly repeated, mentioned in the very first scene of *The Herne's Egg,* can be linked to the endless battles in Yeats's early poem, "The Wanderings of Oisin" (1889), a poem mentioned also in that other recapitulation of his career, "The Circus Animals' Desertion." As usual Yeats, in exploring fresh ideas and material, seems to be rediscovering or confirming what he had long thought and perhaps forgotten.

## COMPOSITION

In the fall of 1935 Yeats was finishing work on his Oxford anthology of modern poetry. The anthology chore proved useful for his own work in at least two ways: he found an inspiring new friend and congenial poetic talent in Lady Dorothy Wellesley, and he looked closely at poetic rhythms. This study of rhythm and the "swift rhythm" of Lady Dorothy's poem "Fire," he wrote to her on 28th November, "have opened my door." In the same letter he tells her that he had "a three-act tragi-comedy in my head . . . not in blank verse but in short line(s) like 'Fire' but a large number of four-stress lines—as wild a play as *Player Queen,* as amusing but more tragedy and philosophic depth."[1] That summer Yeats had received a gift of an oriental lapis lazuli carving. He was already observing it as a symbol of oriental asceticism and gaiety, different from the stubborn, uncompromising world of tragedy. The West, he realized, was the realm of tragedy. The play's tragicomic spirit seems to derive therefore from the mixture of Western with oriental sources.

The Western, specifically Irish, roots of the play took hold as early as 1886 when Yeats read Sir Samuel Ferguson's work and reviewed it in two essays published that year. He had admired then the swift pace of Ferguson's *Congal.* The poem had also probably led him to Ferguson's acknowledged sources, *The Battle of Moyra* (*Cath Muighe Rath*) and *The Banquet of Dunangay* (*Fleadh Dunna n-Gedh*) written down in the fifteenth century by Gilla-Bridghe mac Conmidhe and translated by John O'Donovan from the Irish in 1842.[2] But he did not start to compose the play until November, 1935, when he had it worked out in his head.

1. Wade, 843.
2. See J. P. Frayne, ed., *Uncollected Prose by W. B. Yeats* (London: Macmillan,

─────────────── INTRODUCTION ───────────────

By December 16 he was ensconced in the Hotel Terramar in Palma, working on the prose scenario and then experimenting with sprung rhythm and verse using the prosody of "Fire."

As a letter to his friend the novelist Ethel Mannin shows, on December 20 he hoped to finish as planned "the long detailed scenario of a play, the strangest wildest thing I have ever written."[3] The following day he began his next task: turning his scenario into a verse play. At this early stage he decided not to use sprung rhythm, disliking the "uncertainty as to where the accent falls; it seems to make the verse vague and weak." Yeats preferred "a strong driving force" as the norm, with "a subtle hesitating rhythm" created only where it might be needed. Yeats was clearly enjoying his stay in Palma, working on the play in bed in the morning and then helping Purohit Swami with his translation of *The Upanishads* for an hour each afternoon. He felt the excitement of the creative process and expected his play to produce in him "a new mass of thought and feeling, overflowing into lyrics (these are now in play)."[4] But such was the state of Yeats's health that early in January 1936 heart trouble left him too ill to write.

By April he was feeling better and that month finished his work on *The Upanishads* translation. He still had to write his introduction for the Swami's book. His work on *The Herne's Egg* was under way again during April, as is evident from a letter on April 26 to Olivia Shakespear. On June 30, 1936, Yeats wrote to Lady Dorothy saying that the play would be finished the next day.[5] The lyric outpouring he had hoped for produced "Lapis Lazuli" and other lyrics, written in the immediate aftermath of the play.

The prose scenario and galley proofs are lost. We have, however, MS 8770 in the National Library of Ireland and the carbon copy of a TS version with corrections in Yeats's hand.[6] By August 2, 1937, as we know from a letter to Edith Shackleton Heald, Yeats had finished correcting the proof sheets of the play, which he must have checked during July. The play was published by

---

1970), vol. 1, 81–104; 163 for reference to switch of eggs, showing Yeats knew Gaelic sources. See also *Y and T,* 102, 261.
    3. Wade, 845.      4. Wade, 845–46.
    5. Wade, 854, 858.
    6. This typescript is in the Humanities Research Center, University of Texas; originally submitted to Scribner's with two accompanying sheets of typed corrections for a collection of Yeats's work never in fact published, it is among papers catalogued as: Yeats, W. B., Works, Collected Poetry and Prose.

Macmillan in London early in 1938, for he was sending a copy to Ethel Mannin in February.[7]

When an edition appeared later that year in the United States, Yeats added a preface in which he told his American readers that

> *The Herne's Egg* was written in the happier moments of a long illness that had so separated me from life that I felt irresponsible; the plot echoes that of Samuel Ferguson's *Congal*, and in one form or another had been in my head since my early twenties.

## SOURCES

Following Yeats's hint that the play is Shri Purohit Swami's "philosophy in a fable, or mine confirmed by him,"[8] F. A. C. Wilson stresses the poet's interest in Indian poetry and thought since youth, when he met Mohini Chatterjee and Mme Blavatsky.[9] Yeats saw the *Upanishads* as expressing a subjective philosophy in which mankind is central, finding god in the eternal Self. This is the opposite of the tendency in the later Greek philosophy of Plato and Aristotle, which is more objective, anticipating Christianity with its God to whom all are subservient, the Self and personality being reduced in importance. *The Herne's Egg* draws some of its ideas from India but its characters and setting from the Celtic and Christian past in Ireland. The play also uses the notion of reincarnation, an idea both Indian and Celtic, and the possibility that human souls might be reborn in animal forms of life. The copulation of donkeys just after Congal's death suggests his punishment is to be reborn as a donkey. Attracta's willingness to couple with her servant, Corney, at the end of the play, although she is a priestess, is an attempt to help the dead hero's soul to be reborn as the child she might conceive rather than as an animal. This parallels a Tibetan story Yeats might have been told by his friend Shri Purohit Swami or might have found in Alexandra David-Neel's *With Mystics and Magicians in Tibet* (1931), though this book does not appear in O'Shea's *Catalog* of Yeats's personal library.[10]

---

7. Wade, 894, 904.
8. Wade, 844.
9. See F. A. C. Wilson, *W. B. Yeats and Tradition* (London: Gollancz, 1958), 95–128.
10. See Edward O'Shea, *A Descriptive Catalog of W. B. Yeats's Library* (New York and London: Garland, 1985).

## INTRODUCTION

The story illustrates Tibetan humor. A grand lama, though given every opportunity for learning, passes his life in idleness and can hardly read. He dies. An aged holy man sees a girl near a river and tries to rape her. The girl easily escapes, but her mother sends her back because the saint's actions must have been dictated by some higher good. The girl returns, but he merely shrugs and tells her he had seen the grand lama's spirit drawn toward "a bad rebirth" and had wanted to secure his rebirth in human form. But when she escaped, "the asses in that field nearby coupled. The Grand Lama will soon be reborn as a donkey."[11]

The battle scene which opens the play owes something to Western pantomime and to Chinese opera in its staging; the soldiers' battle is choreographed to music, and mimed without bodily contact as blows are delivered in a stylized symmetrical manner. But there are also literary sources. The fact that fifty battles can be fought with matching blows and wounds for the two kings, Congal and Aedh, suggests that Yeats was remembering *The Mabinogion,* a book that he had read[12] and that influenced the creation of the hero of his early novel, *The Speckled Bird.* In the tale of "Pwyll Lord of Dyved" Arawn instructs Pwyll:

> . . . with one stroke that thou givest him, he shall no longer live. And if he ask thee to give him another, give it not, how much soever he may entreat thee, for when I did so, he fought with me next day as well as ever before.[13]

It may be objected that the motif of magical renewal of an opponent is found in a variety of myths, but we know that Yeats read *The Mabinogion,* and the specific detail of the battle of the two kings rather than of hero and monster, for instance, is near to Yeats's use of the motif.

Another likely source is *The Geeta* (The Gospel of the Lord Shri Krishna).[14] In the dedication "To my friend William Butler Yeats" Shri Purohit Swami noted that "the West has captured the East materially, the East captured the West spiritually, and it is only in Spirit that there has been or can be, meeting. You had vision; you saw truth; you proclaimed it. The East is grateful, the

---

11. Alexandra David-Neel, *With Mystics and Magicians in Tibet* (London: Lane, 1931), 36.
12. In Lady Charlotte Guest's translation (London: Quaritch, 1877).
13. Guest, 341.
14. This book was "put into English" by Shri Purohit Swami and published by Faber & Faber in 1935.

West should be."¹⁵ This exchange of materialism and spiritual wisdom seen in terms of "capture" suggests very clearly the action of *The Herne's Egg*. Congal wages war and captures the spiritual Attracta. By the end of the play he has gained in spirituality and awareness of divinity. She has learned that spirit may work through the material world, incarnated in gross flesh. The battle scene that begins *The Herne's Egg* recalls the battle scene that begins *The Geeta*. Armies are ranged against one another symmetrically, and the text proceeds in short, balanced periods:

> Yet our army seems the weaker, though commanded by Bheeshma, their army seems stronger, though commanded by Bheema.¹⁶

Arjuna, seeing that in battle he must destroy many people, including relatives, friends, and mentors, feels despondent. The Lord Krishna reminds him, however, that spirit is indestructible:

> There was never a time when I was not, nor thou, nor these princes were not; there will never be a time when we shall cease to be.
>
> He who knows the Spirit as Indestructible, Immortal, Unborn, Always-the-same, how should he kill or cause to be killed?
>
> As a man discards his threadbare ashes and puts on new, so the Spirit throws off Its worn-out bodies and takes fresh ones.
>
> Weapons cleave It not, fire burns It not, water drenches It not and wind dries It not.¹⁷

Yeats's play dramatizes this philosophy in its action of punishment through reincarnation, and the battle scene as an image of the way spirit cannot be destroyed: weapons cleave it not. Yeats's warriors in that scene are briefly presented as warring but indestructible souls.

Sir Samuel Ferguson's poem *Congal,* Yeats's main source, was based on the Irish legend of the battle of Moyra, which Yeats could also have read in John O'Donovan's translation (1842); for as Wilson notes, O'Donovan's version contains the detail of substituted eggs (hen's for goose's), not in Ferguson's poem, which Yeats uses as the motive for Congal's lethal attack on Aedh. In the original legend Congal uses the egg insult as a pretext to rebel

15. *Geeta,* 7.  16. *Geeta,* 16.
17. *Geeta,* 21, 22.

against the high king, Domhnall, but is killed later in the battle. In Ferguson's poem, Congal is killed by Cuanna, "an orphan and an idiot."[18] As he dies, he is comforted by Lafinda, his betrothed, who had entered a Christian convent when Congal rebelled against Domhnall. Wilson notes correctly that Yeats lifts and adapts these details for his own dramatic purposes, but adds that Yeats used the Irish legendary framework merely to suggest "a mythological basis for his narrative" so that an audience of "non-initiates" could "take his play at the level of Irish heroic legend." Wilson concludes by overstating his case: "*The Herne's Egg* reflects nothing as much as Yeats's studies with Purohit Swami, and the strain of Irish allusion it contains will not bring us to the heart of his play."[19] This is to ignore a level of meaning at the heart of the action.

Ferguson's introduction to his poem states that he agrees with the view that the legend is concerned with "the expiring effort of the Pagan and Bardic party in Ireland, against the newly-consolidated power of Church and crown."[20] Such a theme and conflict is essentially Yeatsian, the reversal of a historical gyre. Yeats's play, like its comic predecessor *The Player Queen,* dramatizes the turmoil that in Yeats's system always precedes such a reversal. For Yeats, the Bardic age would be subjective or antithetical, the Christian objective, or primary. Yeats presents Congal as objective and Aedh as subjective. In Ferguson's poem, though, Congal leads the subjective Bardic faction against the objective Domhnall, son of Aedh, who had exiled the Bards and permitted "the cleric's grasp on all our fruitful lands."[21] By making his struggle between Congal and Aedh, Yeats refers us back to the pagan and Christian conflict. But in Ferguson it is the Christian king whose followers purloin the hermit Erc's eggs of the wild geese for the banquet. Although Bishop Fonan Finn swears that no insult was intended to Congal when he was given a hen's egg on a wooden instead of silver plate, Congal blasphemously insists his cause for war is right. When Lafinda begs him for peace, Ferguson's Congal replies, "Wars were and will be to the end."[22] This, of course, suggests the eternal nature of war and the fifty battles mentioned in Yeats's first scene. In Ferguson,

---

18. Sir Samuel Ferguson, *Congal, A Poem in Five Books* (Dublin: Ponsonby, 1872), 120.
19. *Y and T,* 104.
20. *Congal,* viii.
21. *Congal,* 6.
22. *Congal,* 41.

# INTRODUCTION

Congal summons British, Saxon, and Frankish aid. Yeats understandably avoids this idea, but he maintains a detail of Congal's character suggested in Ferguson: his rationalism. He also keeps Ferguson's thunderstorm, used in the Victorian poem to destroy the invading fleet, and in Yeats's play to establish fear of the herne god and his judgment. In Ferguson, Lafinda's nurse warns Kellack, a warrior, that "God's angry judgements" may fall "on both soul and limb."[23] In Yeats's play, the pagan god's judgments so fall on Congal and his men. In Ferguson, Congal thanks god for support, although he rarely calls "on any name of God."[24] This differs slightly from Yeats's treatment of Congal as one who does not believe in the herne god until he has been forced by events to do so. Ferguson's anti-clerical thrust becomes in Yeats Congal's heroic and foolish battle against the god. Ferguson's poem ends with the reiteration of his central theme, when after Congal's death Ardan realizes, "I stand alone, / Last wreck remaining of a Power and Order overthrown."[25] Yeats has here his theme of a romanticized Ascendancy overthrown by the new Ireland and his turning of the historical gyre suggested by the ancient struggle of pagan and Christian orders, Bards and Clergy. In Ferguson's notes Yeats could also find suggested the application of Indian material to enrich the theme: Ferguson there cites a *Calcutta Review* article of August 1844 discussing contemporary customs relating to Indian Bhats and Chavans as comparable to the Irish Bards. Both groups had the power to curse and satirize. Both received presents from rulers: an Indian ruler gave his own head as a present, much as Eochaid Einsula gave his one remaining eye to the Scottish bard, Tabhan Draodi.

Another central feature of Yeats's play, the notion of reincarnation, can be found in Egyptian, Greek, Indian, Celtic, and early Christian belief, though, like Yeats, Origen and Tertullian rejected the idea of rebirth of humans in animal form. W. Y. Evans Wentz notes that early Celtic Christians ignored Church councils, which decided against the doctrine of rebirth.[26] The rebirth motif is therefore not an extraneous idea imported from India, but a continuing part of the culture in which the struggle between pagan and Christian cults took place.

23. *Congal*, 62.      24. *Congal*, 76.
25. *Congal*, 147.
26. W. Y. Evans Wentz, *The Tibetan Book of the Dead* (London: Oxford University Press, 1927), 363.

# INTRODUCTION

It might be objected that Yeats's play centers on the challenging of the pagan herne god rather than on a struggle involving Christianity. That would be to ignore, though, the fact that some of the characters have specifically Christian names. We should remember that Yeats, in associating Aedh's kingdom with the herne god and its priestess Attracta, only *seems* to be taking out the Christian elements from his source material. Congal's followers have Christian names, and so do the village girls in the play. These and other points about the Christian elements are more fully discussed later.

Writing to Lady Dorothy Wellesley on May 3, 1936, Yeats remembers that Apuleius in *The Golden Ass* describes a woman having a sexual encounter with a donkey.[27] He also mentions that he is excited mentally and working happily at the play. Apuleius' unfortunate hero, who is turned into an ass, could certainly suggest to Yeats the scallywag Clare highwayman turned into the toy donkey in *The Herne's Egg,* and, of course, Congal's punishment.

A modern Western source is Balzac's *Seraphita*.[28] Yeats's Attracta is based on Balzac's heroine, Seraphita, whose beauty and purity lead her to mystical union with God and the attainment of heaven. The verbal echoes of Balzac's text in the translation Yeats read are clear. Yeats seems to have appropriated snow and ice symbolism associated with Seraphita for his equally pure herne priestess. Seraphita's matchmaking in the village is also shadowed by Attracta's dealing with Kate, Agnes, and Mary. But the most important resemblance is that Seraphita has to resist seven devils to prove her ability to overcome desire. The resemblance is not so complete as Wilson claims, for in Yeats's play Attracta is never tempted, remaining in a trance, oblivious of the men who are intent upon raping her. But both Attracta and Seraphita are changed by their mystical marriages to a condition in which, for Wilson, they are both angelic spirits. In my view, Attracta becomes not an angelic spirit after her union, but a wiser, more human priestess.

Wilson also cites Shakespeare's *Julius Caesar* as a possible source. Brutus, like Congal, surprises and kills his victim; but the treachery of Congal is farcical rather than tragic. Again like

---

27. Wade, 855.
28. Honoré de Balzac, *Seraphita,* trans. Clara Bell (London: Dent, 1897).

# INTRODUCTION

Brutus', Congal's fortunes plummet after the murder, and his end is suicide. Yeats's play, though, offers instead of tragic history only a mode of sacred and profane farce. The gap between the tragic vision and the harsh, satirical vision of *The Herne's Egg* becomes apparent, too, when Yeats adopts briefly the Shakespearean manner in Congal's speech: "I would not have had him die that way / Or die at all, he should have been immortal." But these lines and Pat's brief Antonine oration in this same scene ("let all men know / he was a noble character") are delivered by drunkards.

Yeats's use of source material is highly eclectic and complex. He does not appropriate motifs or ideas without transforming them to contribute to his unique version of the Congal legend. Yeats ensured that the elements discussed above furthered his design of making the struggle of pagan and Christian Ireland a type of the cosmic process he descried in his own age, the ending of one huge historical cycle and the beginning of another.

## CRITICAL DISCUSSION

*The Herne's Egg* was constructed as a stage rather than a salon dance play but during its composition Yeats tightened and abbreviated it from a three-act structure to a short play in six scenes. This achieved greater pace for the action and avoided the necessity of breaking for an interval: the structure of the finished play became a swiftly changing action involving ritual dance movements, passages of crisp dialogue in verse, and crucial moments of flute music and song. Its theatrical style mixes choreographies, words and music, elements capable of expressing stylized comedy, violence, and a remote spirituality.

The action dramatizes the struggle of a new god to emerge in the corner of history that is Ireland at the point of transition from paganism to Christianity. The reversal of the gyre, it seems, does not occur all over the world at the same time. In *Calvary* and *The Resurrection,* Yeats treated the coming of Christian turbulence respectively as an action in Christ's mind and then in its Mediterranean context of pagan religion. In *The Herne's Egg* it is treated in its Irish context. The subjective world of the Great Herne, defended by a Celtic king, Aedh, is coeval with the new dispensation of the objective God, Christ. In making Aedh rather than Domhnall Congal's opponent, Yeats, departing from history, recalled a symbolic persona in his early poetry: there Aedh was "a defeatist lover"[29] telling of perfect beauty, and thus a subjective personality appropriate to the herne's lunar deity. His name, furthermore, means "fire" in Irish, perhaps a subtle reference to Lady Dorothy Wellesley's poem "Fire," the inspiration for Yeats's new brand of dramatic verse.

The battles of perfect equipoise at the beginning of the play suggest the balance of subjective and objective gyres before the squalid events that symbolize the turbulence when one age replaces another. The combat degenerates into drunken brawling and the murder of Aedh with a table leg rather than a real weapon. The single combat expected of a hero at the end instead declines into a sly wounding of Congal by a Fool and then Congal's Roman suicide, which he sees, too late, as merely death at the hands of another fool—himself. These symbolic actions demonstrate the Heraclitean insight that war, conflict, and struggle form the condition of life from which everything arises.[30]

Congal's military conflict with Aedh in the first half of the play becomes a spiritual struggle with Attracta in the second; the entire action is, of course, Congal's struggle with the Herne. The dance for the unsuccessful stoning of the Herne symbolizes this overall conflict and Congal's inevitable defeat. Yeats positions the dance at the point just before the action plunges into the horrors of murder, rape, and suicide.

The play's opposition of subjective and objective eras expresses itself also through the characterization. The subjective Aedh, associated as we have seen with fire, is linked to Attracta though never seen on stage with her. She is a priestess of his kingdom and also is associated with fire. She establishes her spiritual passion when she tells Congal, "I burn / not in the flesh but in the mind." Attracta's use of this metaphor contradicts Congal's imaging of her in terms of ice and snow. Her appetite burns with spiritual rather than fleshly passion. The speech introduces an exalted rhetoric, enhanced by rhyme, of hieratic longing for the sacred marriage of woman and god. Again Yeats departed from his Celtic sources by giving his pagan priestess the Roman name of an early Irish Christian saint. Avoiding the Irish version of her

---

29. See A. N. Jeffares, *W. B. Yeats: Man and Poet* (London: Routledge & Kegan Paul, 1949), 112–14.

30. A. D. Hope in *The Cave and the Spring* (Adelaide: Rigby, 1965), particularly 121–22, discusses military violence in terms relevant to Yeats's drama.

name (Araght), Yeats took her out of her Celtic background, showing again the paradoxical mixture of pagan and Christian elements in this age of transition and stressing the priestess Attracta's saintliness. Yeats wanted his antagonists to make up a symbolic trio with the Fool, in accord with the lunar phases of *A Vision*. Thus Attracta, sacred bride of the herne god, appears at phase twenty-seven (the Saint), Congal, at phase twenty-six (the Hunchback) and the Fool at phase twenty-eight (the Fool). This schema fits their characterization in the play. Moreover, working with the swami and immersed in Asian ideas, Yeats would have thought of those particular phases as appropriate, for in *A Vision* he had surmised, "I think that in Asia it might not be difficult to discover examples at least of phases 26, 27, and 28, final phases of a cycle."[31] And it was appropriate, too, for Yeats to supply examples of personalities belonging to these phases in a play dealing with the end of a cycle. Attracta, when we first see her, has renounced all reality but that of the herne, her god. Her life and movements are controlled by the herne. His tune summons her. When his spirit possesses her she dances as if she were a puppet, the god the puppeteer. When she is raped, her subjective view of that reality prevails: for her it has been the consummation of her marriage to the herne. She is the sacred bride of mythology, and like her she is "all a womb and a funeral urn"; these are the receptacles of life and death, time and timelessness, earthly generation and eternal spirit, paradoxes of the kind discussed by Joseph Campbell.[32] Through rape Attracta will receive the warriors' seed and will later witness Congal's death. The action most shocking to contemporary audiences is thus less shocking to Attracta than Congal's desecration of the herne's eggs. Alienation predominates, as sexuality is used not to express love but to suggest the violence and violation that accompany a reversal of the historical cones.

Yeats, however, does not resolve the ambiguity of the rape, for he introduces after it a changed Attracta. For Congal and the everyday realism of his objective world of disbelief in the herne

31. *Vision*, 177.
32. See *The Hero with a Thousand Faces* (New York: Pantheon, 1961; 1st pub., 1949), 297–314. For the Great Mother's dual nature in its Irish manifestation, see Standish O'Grady, *Silva Gadelica* (New York: Lemma, 1970; London: Williams Norgate, 1892), vol. 2, 370–72.

god, she is now "[a] sensible woman; you gather up what's left." MS 8770 (2) (see "Note on the Text") arrives at an equivalent characterization of Attracta. Yeats's finished play stresses that Attracta has become more of a normal woman. The signs of common humanity in Attracta could lead us to suppose Congal might have been right: rape was "good" for her. Equally, though, it could be that the sacred marriage was "good" for her. But the action does not end with her pregnancy. The herne is at the end of his cycle, and so Attracta does not "lie in a blazing bed" and does not, like the saint of Yeats's poem "The Phases of the Moon," fly like an arrow to heaven from out of the human condition. Before the rape she prays that she might "shoot into my joy." After the rape, her humanity increased, she realizes that for all his power, the god "but begot / His image in the mirror of my spirit, / Being all sufficient to himself / Begot himself; . . ." The next divine birth must be objective, not subjective. It belongs to the Virgin Mary, mother of the opposing cycle.

The dualities of fleshly and spiritual passion explored in Attracta occupied Yeats also in other work of this period, such as his poems and his helping Margot Ruddock with her book *The Lemon Tree* (London: Dent, 1937), for which he wrote an introduction and in which we find images of sexuality and spirituality: "But still my soul / Insatiate / cries out, cries out / For its true mate" (p. 11). In the same volume her poetic persona seems to have a special relationship to the divine: "The Sisters asked me to sing at their shrine and I sang a poem there . . ." (p. 8). Yeats included work of hers in his *Oxford Book of Modern Verse* (1936) as well as poems by Lady Dorothy Wellesley, including "Matrix," in which we read, "The spiritual, the carnal, are one," and "Fire," with its apostrophe to the Earth Goddess, the archetypal sacred bride, "Mother now of all creation, / Guardian, you, of reincarnation, / Who so lately was a bride" and its urgent, somewhat indiscreet question, "Have you wedded flesh to spirit?" (*Oxford Book,* 312, 321). Attracta's rape is ambiguous, being both rape and sacred marriage, thus wedding flesh and spirit. In so far as she is the herne's instrument, she attends not only Congal's death but his conception as a donkey. Linked to his reincarnation, she fails, however, to procure for him a human form in his next life.

The herne's sacred marriage does not make Attracta lay an egg, as Leda did. The substitution of a hen's egg at the banquet indeed suggests the link between the new group religion (hens are gregarious, hernes lonely) and violence, the death of Aedh. The god's egg and the king are both supplanted.

In the scene of the three village girls, more paradoxes obtain. Although living in Aedh's Celtic kingdom, the girls are presented by Yeats as linked to Attracta, yet separate from her, at once fascinated by her position as sacred bride but not themselves fully in tune with such worship: they bear the names Kate, Agnes, and Mary, strongly Christian rather than Celtic or heathen. The three girls form a group, suggesting the collective attributes of objective humanity in Yeats's system, while Attracta remains separate from them, soon retreating into her subjective trance under the influence of her god. The presents the girls bring to Attracta suggest a parody of the presents brought to the infant god, Christ. Attracta possibly sees that Mary will also become a sacred bride when she tells her "Mary shall be married / When I myself am married / To the lad that is in her mind."

Typical of the play is the ambiguity of these lines. Attracta is light-heartedly teasing Mary by not naming this "lad"—we know who he is, but we are not saying. At the same time, the lines suggest that Mary is intended for someone "in her mind" rather as the Virgin Mary in Christian iconography is impregnated by a bird with rays of light entering her head. Mary is an analogue of the Mary who brings a new god, a new era. Mary's marriage will not precede but coincide in some way with Attracta's and the lad that is in Mary's mind is the ideal, the spirit, not a village lover. Among the girls, it is Mary alone who has seen Attracta twice before in a trance, and understands that at such moments her "human life is gone / And that is why she seems / A doll upon a wire." Mary's connection with Attracta marks her off, then, as another sacred bride. And if we do not notice this connection, we miss the point of the inclusion of the village girls into the play. Basically, of course, they are a plot mechanism to get the hen's egg to Attracta for substitution at the banquet. But if this were all, they would be merely a device. Yeats uses them also to comment, choruslike, on Attracta's possession and dance. Mary's role as analogue of an objective sacred bride then draws the episode into place with the pagan and Christian threads in the fabric of the play.

Yeats also connects Mary with the little hen's egg Attracta substitutes for the herne's egg at the banquet, thus precipitating the main action:

## INTRODUCTION

> MARY   She has still my little egg.
> AGNES   Who knows but your little egg comes into some mystery?
> KATE   Some mystery to make love-loneliness more sweet?

Mary's sacred role emerges, too, in Agnes's speculation and Kate's response. At the level of action the hen's egg is indeed at the center of the mystery of this play. The substitution of "objective" egg for "subjective" egg is at once a trigger for and a parody of the changing of the gyres, the replacement of one age by another.

In the course of revision, Yeats altered Jane (in the MS version) to Kate, moved the "bridal torch" lines to spark the argument between Agnes and Kate, and added new lines for Mary, so that her line about "my little egg" becomes the end of an important ten-line speech. But in having Mary talk about *her* egg, Yeats introduces a confusion, for it was Kate, not Mary, who brought the hen's eggs on stage. Perhaps, in writing the scene, Yeats became excited by the notion of making Mary a reflection of the Christian Virgin, and forgot to go back in the scene to adjust the gift bearing. He may, on the other hand, deliberately have left the confusion in order to suggest irrational mystery and undermine attempts to allegorize the scene, for the realization that not Mary but Kate brought the eggs prompts a parallel: Kate has brought hen's eggs, which Mary thinks of as hers, just as Corney has herne's eggs which Attracta regards as hers. Yet whether Yeats nodded or deliberately confused us, it is Mary who has the last word in the scene. Her last lines are prophecy, asserting the mystic marriage of Attracta to a Zeus-like god. Mary among the three girls certainly comes closest to Attracta's vision of events. Mary's vision of Attracta as bride is powerful and direct, foreshadowing Attracta's own account later on. Mary's knowledge singles her out, then, as a likely successor to Attracta as a type of sacred bride, though not, as we have seen, a bride of the herne. Another ambiguity in the scene is that Agnes and Kate suggest saints associated with the Virgin Mary: at the same time, in Yeats's day they were common enough names for Catholic servants in Anglo-Irish Protestant houses. The defeated Ascendancy class can readily be represented by the lonely, distinguished culture of King Aedh. In Aedh's society, like that of the Ascendancy, Yeats shows subservient Catholics whose time is at hand: they will soon be in control. The cycles of history hold their own ironies.

If we remember that Mary, like Christ, rode on a donkey, the episode of the village girls relates thematically to the donkey image that runs through the play and provides its comic curtain line. Read in this way, the girls' brief episode fits the play's action more than at first seems possible. The girls resemble the chorus in Yeats's earlier dance plays, but are lightly characterized: Agnes is curious about the physicality of Attracta's sacred marriage; Kate is practical, eager to show their offerings; Mary has knowledge and speculation about the mystical life of Attracta. Finally, the scene uses the credulity of the three girls—with their excited reactions to Attracta's trance, their belief in her prophetic powers, and their spirited speculations about her sacred marriage—to establish very firmly in the minds of an audience the possibility that Attracta is indeed what she is claimed to be. This makes a fitting preparation for the theatricality of Attracta's dance.

Nevertheless, we expect some further development of the three to emphasize the clash of Christian with pagan. But it is clear Yeats was concerned to stress the general struggle between a waning subjective era and an objective one taking over, rather than the specific conflict between druids and church found in Ferguson's *Congal*.

Congal is at phase twenty-six of Yeats's moon symbolism—the phase of "The Multiple Man" or Hunchback. This puts him in opposition to the humpbacked bird god. Head of a gang, he is indeed "Multiple Man." As Yeats tells us, "If he live amid a theologically minded people, his greatest temptation may be to defy God. . . ."[33] Congal brings the curse of the herne on himself by purloining the eggs and desecrating the sanctuary. In the stoning scene he continues his defiance, as he also intends with the rape. Congal's refusal at first to kneel in the thunder scene continues his opposition; from one point of view he is heroic, from another merely obtuse. J. Rees Moore sees that Congal "comes late and reluctantly to an understanding (if it can truly be called that) of the mission incumbent on him to establish contact with godhead. He is duly punished for his recalcitrance."[34] In the thun-

---

33. *Vision*, 178.
34. J. Rees Moore, *Masks of Love and Death: Yeats as Dramatist (Ithaca: Cornell Univ. Press, 1971)*, 55. See also *Com. Pl.*, 271, note 669.

der scene, the comedy intensifies when Congal on his knees confesses in a circuitous way to fear of thunder. Here, momentarily again, is Congal's rational view of events, akin to his earlier explanation of Attracta as merely a frustrated woman.

Congal's sensuality and coarse wit (part of the "forced bonhomie"[35] Yeats found in men of phase twenty-six) appear in several places. He deliberately breaks one taboo against handling the eggs, and by having them cooked he defies another. With savage irony, part of his punishment at the end of the play proves to be impalement on a cooking spit. The play's culinary motif develops quickly into the banquet imagery and ends with the stage business and properties used for Congal's death scene.

That a Fool wounds Congal refers not only to the Celtic sources and Ferguson's *Congal* but also to the Fools of Yeats's early plays, *On Baile's Strand* and *The Hour Glass*. Congal dies defiant as ever, but the herne has not finished with him. Although he tries to assert and demonstrate heroic qualities, the fact remains that Congal thinks of the cowardly rape as "winning" a bout with the herne, and this action, together with the fear of the bird in the court scene and Congal's grotesque and ill-considered suicide, certainly align him more closely with the rapscallion donkey—and Yeats's farcical fable thus achieves effective satire of his central character.

Mike is the first to specify the number of rapists as seven. Several theories about the significance of rape by seven have been offered. One was that they represented the seven sacraments, another that they are the seven deadly sins. F. A. C. Wilson suggests that Congal is passion and the soldiers are the six specific sins linked to passion in the Upanishads (vanity, jealousy, sloth, anger, greed, and lust). Yeats does not characterize the soldiers in a way that fits in with these theories, as Jeffares has pointed out.[36]

At several points in the play, their number is given as seven, i.e., Congal and six followers as listed in all editions of the play: the soldiers Mike, Pat, Malachi, Mathias, Peter, and John.[37] In stage directions and in attributing lines, though, Yeats names one more soldier, James. This character is unlisted in all printings of

---

35. *Vision*, 178.
36. *Com. Pl.*, 269.
37. For a fuller discussion than what follows, see my note, "The Case of the Eighth Rapist," *Canadian Journal of Irish Studies* 10, no. 1 (June 1984), 127–31.

## INTRODUCTION

the text[38] and, there is no list of *dramatis personae* in MS 8770 or the *Scribner's TS*. In preparing the list for the published version of the play, Yeats or his editor either inadvertently or deliberately omitted to include James. The confusion runs deeper, since in scene 4, when the soldiers are contemplating the rape of Attracta, both Malachi and James have lines to speak. When Congal names the seven rapists he omits Peter, who had entered with Congal at line 40; but in scene 5 Peter is among those who brag that they had raped Attracta the night before. And despite Malachi's being named specifically in scene 4 among the rapists, and as present in scene 5, he does not there confirm his part in the rape.

Thus at one point or another there are, including Congal, eight named rapists; and Yeats makes it impossible simply to cut out one of the names, double up a part and reduce the eight men to the oft-mentioned seven, unless one wants to reattribute lines of dialogue or change or ignore a name mentioned in stage directions for entrances. This seems to weigh against mere carelessness in the revision or proof-reading stage. We have no real solution to the problem. Yeats was weak, convalescent, and as usual overworked when he was writing *The Herne's Egg*; confusion over who brought the eggs and the number of soldiers could be errors on his part, for we have no proof that they were deliberate. And yet Yeats admitted he wrote the play in an irresponsible mood. As his sense of humor was a subtle one, there remains at least an element of doubt.

There is no doubt, however, as to the deft, economical touches by which Yeats characterizes realistically rather than allegorically *all seven* of Congal's soldiers. Malachi is named as one of the rapists, but he has promised his mother that he would avoid women. He neither admits to participation in the rape nor denies it. He may be more afraid of his mother than of the herne. John, by contrast, is a married man with a jealous wife. James is genteel and conventionally aware of social shame. He fears that his fiancée and her family will discover his part in the rape. He is sadistic, being the first to suggest Attracta must be punished by death. He also takes note of what his mother tells him. Mathias, on the other hand, is said by Congal to be a "coarse hunk of clay." This goes well with his superstitious fear of Attracta. He watches her closely and is the first to notice that the eggs have been switched.

---

38. *Variorum*, 1012.

# INTRODUCTION

Pat has the most obviously Irish idiom in his speeches and is also the leading drunk in the drinking scene, being given a soliloquy and much maudlin talk. Peter is the most shadowy of the soldiers. He boasts of having raped Attracta, but is not specifically named by Congal. He is the obvious soldier to cut in production in order to bring their numbers down to six. Mike's terse interjections characterize him as a military, secular counterpart of oracular advice. He is like a trusted N.C.O., an aspect of Congal's consciousness until the last scene, where Congal has resolved to meet his fate. Mike foresees the violence and horror to come. We should also remember that terse, riddling speech was a feature of the mnemonics used in the training of the Celtic bards.[39] Mike, as Congal's right hand man, is a counterpart of Attracta's donkey-handler, Corney. Where Mike is curt and military, Corney is loquacious and humorous. He makes sure that the Donkey, in itself an effective stage property, becomes more; he ensures it lives as a character as well as a symbol of the objective dispensation which replaces that of the subjective herne.

Symbols from some previous works by Yeats are revived in *The Herne's Egg*. We have already seen that the characterization includes symbolic personalities from *A Vision* (Hunchback, Saint, and Fool) and that the herne, like the heron of *Calvary*, is the type of a subjective deity. But it is worth mentioning that by putting bird and donkey together in the same play with the sacred figure of Attracta, Yeats is echoing Christian religious iconography. In some medieval illuminated books and religious paintings of the Italian renaissance the heron was an emblem of virtuous vigilance.[40] Bellini's *St. Francis* (Frick Collection) depicts a heron and a donkey near the saint. Yeats, though, was using his emblematic bird in a pagan rather than Christian way. But the donkey as herald of a new era is Yeatsian and Christian. Enjoying such precedents and connections, Yeats used the symbolism very theatrically: that the donkey should be a life-size toy makes for a wonderful stage effect, establishing a carnival mood after the battle scene. It also introduces the notion of metempsychosis, or the passage of the soul after death from one animal body to another,

---

39. See John Sharkey, *Celtic Mysteries* (London: Thames and Hudson, 1975) 13: "Riddles and sophisticated word-play are a reminder of the origin of all sacred mysteries: Breath, or the Word itself."

40. See Louis Réau, *Iconographie de l'art chrétien* (Paris: Presses Universitaires de France, 1955–59), 3 vols.

# INTRODUCTION

in a jocular manner acceptable to a modern audience unlikely to take such an idea seriously. Yeats used the transmigration of souls as part of his plan to express Shri Purohit Swami's "philosophy in a fable, or mine confirmed by him;"[41] it would have pleased Yeats that both Indian and Celtic belief accepted the doctrine.[42]

Similarly, the egg symbol is both Indian and Celtic. As Melchiori has shown,[43] it is the cosmic egg, the sum of reality. In the Celtic sources a goose egg was disputed, and was thus a symbol of discord. Yeats's heron's egg owes something to each of these.

In keeping with the mood of his play and its elements of parody and satire, Yeats makes fun of his own most serious symbols. The elaborate moon symbolism he worked out in *A Vision* and used in *A Full Moon in March* he spoofs with a comic pantomime moon for Congal's death at the end of the play. The cooking utensils and stone, those "props" of the Fool, are parodies of the stone of destiny, and the precious symbols of Yeats's youthful dreams of a castle of the Heroes:[44] the cauldron of the Dagda, the Golden Spear of Victory, and Lugh, the Sword of Light. The transformation of these symbols seems analogous to the transformation of one age into another, and of man into beast. Indeed, we might say of the symbols of this play what Yeats said of those in *A Vision*: "[A]ll the symbolism of this book applies to begetting and birth, for all things are a single form which has divided and multiplied in time and space."[45] The prime example of that process is the egg. *The Herne's Egg* is about the struggle of the modern, and the struggle of any age, to be born.

## VERSIFICATION AND DRAMATURGY

The printed versions of the play show that Yeats, as he explained in the letters already cited, had discovered a new, flexible, yet regular versification for his stage. His experiment led to the style used in *Purgatory* that Eliot praised as a true vehicle for modern

---

41. Wade, 844.
42. As A. H. Leahy noted long ago, "Transmigration or re-birth, that element of Celtic belief which drew the attention of the ancient world, is of frequent occurrence; in some tales this idea is the principal motive of the story . . ." (*The Courtship of Ferb* [London: Nutt, 1902] no. xvii).
43. *WMA*, 64–199.
44. See A. N. Jeffares, *W. B. Yeats: Man and Poet* (London: Routledge & Kegan Paul, 1962; 1949), 140. When Congal impales himself, if the actor falls across the stone, it becomes an altar, he its human sacrifice to the herne and, for a moment, the god's unwitting priest.
45. *Vision*, 212.

speech in verse drama.[46] The poetic line in *The Herne's Egg* accommodates the mixture of three and four stresses per line for the opening dialogue between Congal and Aedh, giving a terse, colloquial effect. The prevailing four-stress lines that appear in scene 2 and the rest of the play can achieve very strong rhythms, as in Corney's soliloquy that opens scene 2 and describes the toy donkey in a four-stress line similar to the old butcher's rhyme.[47] The verse can also render the simple but lofty formalities of Attracta's speech; the arrogance and self-satisfaction of Congal's talk; the conversational tone adopted by Attracta when she meets the three girls at the end of scene 2; the lyric quality of the curse and Attracta's song, "When I take a beast to my joyful breast." (No music for the play appeared during Yeats's lifetime, but in production it would afford opportunities for humor, lyricism, and atmosphere.)

The song has a number of functions. It establishes a state of mind in Attracta that is no longer a deep trance, yet is remote from the ordinary waking world of drunken soldiers. It provides a suitably stylized vocal accompaniment to the ritual of the caps. It demonstrates an elevated spiritual interpretation of the imminent carnal act, directly at odds with its being gang rape. Its refrain, being cast in the third person, contrasts with the first person usage of the verses, and thus serves to remind us that Attracta sings of events that pertain to a traditional figure, "the bride of the Herne," who is represented by Attracta on this occasion. Finally, the song is a prothalamium that asserts a spiritual purity that survives intercourse, a joy that also knows terror, and an uncertainty about the effects of intercourse. The last three lines stress the humanity and pathos of the sacred bride who is little more than a girl. The prothalamium closes the scene effectively, giving a sense of order transcending the disorder of Congal and his men, who, ironically, are trying to establish an order among themselves by a test involving skill and luck. But in Yeats's view (as in *Calvary* for

---

46. T. S. Eliot, *Poetry and Drama* (London: Faber and Faber, 1951), 20. See also his "The Poetry of W. B. Yeats" in James Hall and Martin Steinman, eds., *The Permanence of Yeats* (New York: Collier Books, 1961), 303–5. Eliot, correct about *Purgatory*, ignored the fact that its verse derived from the experimental versification of *The Herne's Egg*.

47. "A rump steak, a leg off the loin, / Up the middle and down the chine! / Three, four, half a pound / And if you want your meat, Lady, / Take the baby's bum off the counter!"

instance) what appears to men as chance may be the working of God's will, or choice.

The four-stress line here is well suited to the rhythm of folk song. With the sole exception of the last line, all the lines of Attracta's song, including its six-stress refrain, fall into two halves. This allows for an easy breathing pattern for any singer, so long as the musical setting is like a folk tune rather than anything more elaborate. The two-part lines establish a pattern in the song that is broken by the unity of the last line, "Shall I be the woman lying there?" But musically the line asks to be repeated, thus completing the two-part pattern established by the preceding lines. Though not necessary, such a repetition could serve two purposes: it could give the audience time to reflect on the ambiguity of the word "lying" and give emphasis to what is, after all, a curtain line.

In general, the short lines avoid the oddities to be found in the long lines of Yeats's earlier heroic farce, *The Green Helmet,* allowing instead brisk, effective stage dialogue and generally simple diction. This is colloquial, often monosyllabic, and by no means literary or archaic. Yet as befits the setting in the remote past, the words avoid the modern catch phrases or contemporary clichés found in realistic prose plays. Yeats employed stage diction here capable of expressing dignity, formality, informality, drunkenness, and the entire emotional range of his action.

The decision to simplify his poetic line leads to a strong, uncluttered syntax. It also accords with his decision to pare down the play's structure from three acts to six scenes. These six scenes have an abundance of theatrical and dramatic energy. The stylized battle that begins the play could, in the hands of a good director and choreographer, be a theatrical *tour de force* in the manner of Chinese or Japanese warrior scenes. Similarly, the stoning and swordplay directed at the invisible herne in scene 3 has great potential for stage movement. Then Yeats gives us a deliberate contrast in the drunken brawl in which Aedh is murdered. This scene and the drunken talk that follows offer a great deal to the actors. In contrast to group violence, Congal's lonely suicide beneath the smile of a comic moon has a different but powerful effect. The choreography of violence finds its opposite in the serene movements of Attracta and her stylized dance of the sacred and profane eggs. This dramatically effective use of contrasting scenes gives thematic emphasis and offers opportunities for bold

# INTRODUCTION

strokes of characterization. For example, Yeats contrasts the "trial" of Attracta by Congal with the herne's "trial" of Congal in the thunder scene. The two scenes allow Yeats to bring out the swagger and sadistic impulses of the soldiers, as well as some of their insecurities, and then to show their cowardice and fear, when after the rape they have to face retribution. Congal alone emerges from the thunder scene as a man of real courage. Mike, his terse adviser earlier in the play, is of no further use.

The power and presence of the herne make themselves felt in a number of theatrical ways: the music and songs; the mime of Congal and his men in their attacks on the elusive bird with stones and swords; the trance state and movements (including the dance) of Attracta; the sound of thunder. But most profoundly of all, we have to believe that the herne is a pagan god, because the actress playing Attracta must believe it and convey that faith and conviction to us. This effect has to be reinforced by Corney and by Congal and his men, who abandon their skepticism for belief in the existence and power of the herne god.

The endings of the six scenes also are strong and varied in effect. Scene 1 ends with Aedh's jocular, absurd laugh line about the lazy dog, just as scene 6 ends the play with Corney's musing on the absurdity of Congal as another animal, the donkey. In contrast, scene 2 closes with the ecstatic lyricism of the three girls, struck with awe at the thought of the god as lover. Scene 3, however, finishes on a lower key, with a laugh line, which yet seems to be foreboding, as Congal's teeth are set on edge by the tune, "The Great Herne's Feather." The ending of scene 4 provides yet another contrast. It brings the play to a major dramatic climax and a complex emotional effect. The climax is the decision to rape Attracta. Suddenly the motionless virgin bursts into song, staring straight ahead of her, while the soldiers throw their caps to see who shall violate her first. The stage holds two moods in violent conflict with each other. Properly staged this climax achieves a powerful poetry of the theater. Scene 5, in which the followers of Congal are reduced to comic, cowardly louts, ends with a quieter dramatic effect: Congal's moment of heroic choice, his decision to meet Attracta and his fate on the mountainside. Yeats gives him honesty and moral courage; for him, a different kind of heroic line: "Because I am terrified, I will come."

With good acting, these effects will be powerful, convincing statements that make the play work as a dramatic realization of the violent changeover from one kind of society and ethos to another. If acting cannot convince us to accept the herne imaginatively, then Yeats's lines, however powerful themselves, cannot work properly, and all we are left with is the basic fable of a disreputable gang of armed men who murder and rape on the pretext of an insult. This may be true to the more hideous movements in the melancholy history of mankind, but to be interesting as drama, the rape would have to carry with it insight into and analysis of the action from moral, human, and social perspectives. The Yeatsian perspective of a system of historical cycles and the immortality of the human soul functions in a similar way if it can be made convincing to the audience. One can argue that modern audiences might be more in tune with such ideas than were Yeats's contemporaries, but the task of making the Yeatsian ethos clear and convincing in the theater remains with the director and cast.

## PRODUCTION AND CRITICAL RECEPTION

Yeats sent his play to the Abbey Theatre in 1936. By late November of that year he had heard that a production of *The Herne's Egg* was scheduled for the early spring of 1937, and he predicted "there would be an uproar."[48] But then the Abbey board of Governors rejected the play. Frank O'Connor left an account of this decision, and Hugh Hunt, director at the Abbey 1935–38, recalls that Yeats offered him the play, which he declined, whereupon Yeats "held out *Purgatory* as an alternative."[49] Annoyed by the Abbey's rejection, Yeats offered the play to the Mercury Theatre. Ashley Dukes and Martin Browne considered it along with others by Yeats late in 1936, but they did not produce it.[50] The play was first staged by Austin Clarke's Lyric Theatre Company, which gave two performances with settings by Anne Yeats at the Abbey Theatre, Dublin, on October 29 and November 5, 1950. It has seldom been professionally staged since, but notable performances in Ireland include: Mary O'Malley's successful and widely reviewed production of a triple bill with *The Cat and the Moon* and

48. Wade, 868.
49. See Frank O'Connor, "Quarreling with Yeats: A Friendly Recollection," *Esquire* 62, no. 6 (December 1964) reprinted in E. H. Mikhail, ed., *W. B. Yeats: Interviews and Recollections* (London: Macmillan, 1977), 339–45. Hugh Hunt's remark comes from his letter to Andrew Parkin, dated May 9, 1982.
50. See Richard J. Finneran, George Mills Harper, and William M. Murphy, eds., *Letters to W. B. Yeats* (London: Macmillan, 1977), vol. 2, 587.

─────────── INTRODUCTION ───────────

*The Resurrection* during the first week of June 1964 at the Lyric Theatre, Belfast; the successful double bill of *Purgatory* and *The Herne's Egg* at the Peacock Theatre, Dublin, on September 14, 1973, directed by Jim Fitzgerald; and the Lyric Theatre, Belfast, production in a double bill with *The Shadowy Waters* which opened on August 21, 1979, directed by James Flannery.

Because publication of the play in 1938 preceded stage production, the earliest reactions are those of book reviewers. Responses were usually unfavorable, ranging from abuse in the *Catholic Bulletin* to the *Dublin Review*'s frosty assertion, "The amours of a super-heron are neither edifying nor amusing."[51] The *Times Literary Supplement,* publishing the first review to appear, set the tone for serious treatment of the play by noting its "extravagant fancies," its "irreverent appeal," and found the central themes to be "animal vigour" and reincarnation.[52] Austin Clarke reviewed it for the *New Statesman,* telling his readers that Yeats's "new extravaganza" attempted "the madcap spirit of the old mock-heroic tales of Gaelic tradition," but that its verse was "small beer";[53] in a later *London Mercury* review, Clarke went deeper, discovering the ambiguity by which the serious was instantly "revealed as absurdity" in an interesting blend of "symbolic fantasy" with "comic realism," which also achieved through Congal a Yeatsian satire of militarism.[54] Clarke's deeper understanding of the play eventually resulted, one suspects, in his decision to test it in stage production.

The most searching notice appeared in the *Yale Review,* where Kerker Quinn ranked *The Herne's Egg,* "by virtue of its novelty, sharp characterization, and enchanting lines, among the four or five best he [Yeats] has ever written." But he qualified his praise because of the "strange and perverse symbolism" that obscured the meaning.[55] He saw the play as coming close to surrealism. The most distinguished reviewer, Edmund Wilson, writing in the *New Republic,* saw the piece as "a fantasy on the Leda theme" in which, as in *The King of the Great Clock Tower* and *A Full Moon in March,* a "cold but beautiful" woman first destroys

51. *Catholic Bulletin* (Dublin), 28, no. 3 (March 1938), 185–86; *Dublin Review* 202, no. 405 (April–June 1938), 387–88.
52. *YTCH,* 394–95.
53. *YTCH,* 397–98.
54. "A Stage Fantasy," *London Mercury* 37, no. 221 (March 1938), 551–52.
55. "Through Frenzy to Truth," *Yale Review* 27, no. 4 (Summer 1938), 834–36.

a lover, then "comes under his spell." He concluded that Yeats was "still a great writer" because his art was Protean, and that in *The Herne's Egg* he had found a new homeliness and humor that made his work less trancelike.[56]

In *Life and Letters Today*, however, George Barker praised Yeats for his passion and "magnificent manipulation of words," finding "most expert and extraordinary the way in which the words come and move and militate." This sensitivity to Yeats's poetic diction was matched in his review by a courageous admission that the scene in which the sentence of rape is passed on Attracta "is conspicuously fine." The weakness of the play for Barker is that the mythic material is "anaemic." His judgment on "a grand if erratic poet" is delivered with some wit: "And against the nothing less than superb humanity of the king and his soldiers, the Herne looks a trifle taxidermic."[57]

*The Herne's Egg,* then, aroused the distaste of some of Yeats's contemporaries as it has of some modern critics, most prominently Helen Vendler and Harold Bloom. Vendler, among the most interesting and lucid of critics, dismisses the play as drama and offers an aesthetic reading in which the Herne is the Muse/Daimon, Attracta the poet—because she sings—and the Egg the poem.[58] The problem with this reading is that it ignores the other dimensions, especially the themes arising from Yeats's treatment of his main source, *Congal*. Bloom's attack is the most pungent and outspoken since those in the Irish Catholic press of 1938. While his comments admit the play's power, they make some serious charges which should be faced.

Bloom argues that Yeats's play suffers from mixing farce with visionary experience, that it is squalid, for the conflict of self and soul "grows progressively more sordid" and that the squalor is symptomatic of a larger fault, "the mounting confusion and systematic inhumanity of the last phase of Yeats." The confusion Bloom detects boils down to a number of issues, all linked to Yeats's refusal either to confirm or deny his own "myth of reality."[59] But the holding of doubt and certainty in balance is the strength of Yeats's dramatic action. Reality is at best a problematic

---

56. *New Republic* 95, no. 1230 (June 29, 1938), 226.
57. *Life and Letters Today* 18, no. 11 (Spring 1938), 173.
58. *Yeats's Vision and the Later Plays* (Cambridge: Harvard Univ. Press, 1963), 158–67.
59. *Yeats* (New York: Oxford Univ. Press, 1970), 422.

concept; metaphysical speculation makes it elusive and not open to materialistic interpretation only. Yeats's lifelong grappling with the evidence and lack of evidence for the existence and immortality of the soul made him well aware of the way in which a set of facts might bear simultaneously a materialistic and a nonmaterialistic interpretation. It is this ambiguity he dramatized in *The Herne's Egg*. Congal encounters a "subjective" deity in which he cannot believe and ends by committing suicide, having come to believe in the reality of the herne god. Attracta believes in this reality throughout. The audience's beliefs are another matter entirely. Agnostics or atheists may interpret the action in a materialistic way, but they cannot deny that Attracta has the unswerving belief that she serves a god, and that her rape was a mystic marriage to that god. Nor can they deny that Congal and his men start as unbelievers and finish as believers thoroughly convinced the god is out to punish them. Furthermore, perceptive atheists versed in Yeats's system could detect that through the donkey symbolism in the play, the action dramatizes the violence and horror that accompany the change from one historical gyre to another. Attracta's stubborn refusal to admit her rape is at once mystical and a piece of profound psychological insight. In realistic terms it is her defense mechanism. Thus the play works on a realistic level. As for the supernatural level, many people believe in reincarnation, and a great many more can entertain the idea, much as they play with astrology, to the extent that they accept it for the purposes of the play. Bloom thinks Attracta "silly and debased" at the end of the play; he dislikes her willingness to copulate with a donkey-handler. But Corney is a means to a spiritual end and a sympathetic character. His astonishment at her urgency is part of the scene's humor. Finally, Bloom disapproves of what he thinks of as the militarism of the play, astutely noting that Aedh's idea of the fifty battles as being "perfect" is typical of the military mind. But Yeats was dramatizing at once a turbulent period of warring chieftains and the violence he saw as always accompanying the shifts in historical gyres. Accepting the inevitability of violence, he satirizes the warriors and parodies his own previous work and symbolism in a satirical way. At the reversal of the gyres, everything is called in doubt except the ineluctable historical process. That is what Yeats's play demonstrates.

John Rees Moore also describes *The Herne's Egg* as a parody of Yeats's "own heroic dramas."[60] His account of the later Yeats's stripping down of myth is lucid and convincing. Rather than confusion at the end of the play, Moore finds Yeatsian irony "remarkably balanced, implying at least as much ridicule of those who would make a donkey of Congal as of Congal himself." The play gives no assurances of a benign universe, but shows "that the pain of life can only be made to yield dignity if we view ourselves with a kind of detached passion, realizing how near akin folly and wisdom are."

The basic strategy of "combining sophistication and naiveté" in the "comic stylization of primitive material" was something Yeats had already discovered in *The Green Helmet* and Eliot in *Sweeney Agonistes*.

Moore sees at once the organizing principle of *The Herne's Egg*: "The same action regarded from a "tough," pragmatic standpoint and then from a "noble," transcendent one. Both views are reduced to logical absurdity by deflation" (p. 284). He argues cogently that "the play offers Yeats's most complex analysis of the heroic dilemma" (p. 296) and that within its "mythical framework" it presents "a view of the supernatural at once so austere and so fantastic that we may well honour Congal" for struggling against a divine creature that is "arbitrary, vengeful, terrifying, cruel, and absurd" (pp. 297–98). Moore does not discuss the source materials so thoroughly treated by Wilson and amended by Bloom; instead, he discusses the implications of the play's strategy and action, giving the fullest and best account of the key speeches and the dramatic force of the play.

Brenda S. Webster applies psychoanalysis to Yeats's work to find what brings no surprises—that Yeats in old age reasserted his sexual potency in order to combat decay and the approach of death. Her best insight is that Attracta assumes a maternal aspect after the rape, in that she is willing to become Congal's mother.[61]

Bernard G. Krimm offers a reading of the play in which the opening battle is a reference to the civil strife in Ireland in the twenties and thirties. Congal represents de Valera. War has sapped the riches of the country, and in stealing the eggs (future promise) Congal-de Valera is robbing future generations. Attracta is the fertile spirit of Ireland. The punishment of Congal and his men

---

60. *Masks of Love and Death,* 52–56.
61. *Yeats: A Psychoanalytic Study* (Stanford: Stanford Univ. Press, 1973).

by rebirth into a lower form of life suggests a hideously bestial future for Irish politics. He concludes that "the play reveals Yeats's mastery in shaping the ancient myth of Congal into a piece of political satire suitable to the turmoil of twentieth century Ireland."[62] It is unlikely that Yeats would write a political allegory, since his usual practice was to avoid allegory in his writing. But this does not preclude any political significance in the play; Walter Starkie pointed out in his 1938 essay, "Ireland Today," that the Irish had been watching since 1922 "the birth of an infant state" and some would inevitably recall the idea that the new state was like "a physical body prepared for the incarnation of the soul of a race."[63] Yeats's work suggests that such incarnations are the result of rape and outrage. *The Herne's Egg* dramatizes that outrage and suggests that the body of the new state will be like a donkey containing the soul of man. It is in this satirical and mischievous spirit that Yeats's play is political. Very specific political readings seem to me difficult to establish convincingly and are too restrictive to fit the usual Yeatsian manner. Krimm's political key does not negotiate all the wards.

Richard Cave's lecture to the British Academy in September 1982 argues that Yeats's last three plays dramatize the struggle between man and gods in terms indebted to his translation of Sophocles' *King Oedipus*. Yeats adapts the Sophoclean scheme by which Apollo controls events and forces Oedipus to recognize "who is master of his fate."[64] In his last three plays, Yeats creates characters whose struggles with supernatural forces reveal the naked self. Attracta totally upsets Congal's view of reality. Yet his impact on her is such that she feels incomplete. If she has awakened a sense of the spiritual in Congal, he has made her face the reality of suffering. Although played under "the moon of comic tradition," the last scene, in Cave's view, subtly substitutes pathos for laughter, for Yeats gives "some human worth to Congal and Attracta that survives the ridicule" (pp. 311–12). The play offers a series of paradoxes, so that nothing is what it seems at first.

Richard Taylor treats *The Herne's Egg* as expressing Yeats's "religio-philosophical vision" in an original structure which is more elaborate and complex than that of "any of his earlier

---

62. *W. B. Yeats and the Emergence of the Irish Free State* (Troy, NY: Whitson Publishing Co., 1981), 184.
63. *Quarterly Review* 271: 538 (October 1938): 343–60.
64. *Proceedings of the British Academy* 68 (1982): 299ff.

works."⁶⁵ But then Taylor proceeds to give an allegorical reading of the play that does not do full justice to its complexity. The soldiers are not characterized in such a way as to represent the various qualities with which allegorizing critics like to label them. The same argument applies to Attracta's three girl companions. Taylor's discussion of the Fool in terms of Congal's antiself and as a counterpart for Judas in *Calvary* is much more helpful. Moreover, Taylor is the only critic to discuss the significance of the gestation period of the donkey.⁶⁶ He remarks that the gestation period is normally twelve not thirteen months. By insisting on thirteen months, Yeats was reminding us of his theory of the thirteenth cone—a state of pure spirit and freedom from the cycles of temporal existence. Taylor is also right in suggesting that the last words of the play are ironic—the action has more to show for it than just another donkey, for the play suggests that a new era is at hand, the antithesis of the herne's subjective era. Finally, Taylor usefully summarizes the pattern of antitheses established in the play: sun and moon, beast and bird, stone and egg, the arming and disarming of warriors, love and war, chance and choice.

The most recent major consideration of *The Herne's Egg* is that of Alison Armstrong, who reads the ironic treatment of sexuality as symbolic of the marriage of contraries, or primary and antithetical tinctures.⁶⁷ Congal and Attracta represent these contraries and both are subservient to the Great Herne. Both are changed by experience, Congal finding his mask in defeat. Both find that self-knowledge comes from the struggle with unpredictable authority. Congal's own decree that a balance must be struck is ironically confirmed but at a level beyond his knowledge. Armstrong treats the play as a major achievement and has transcribed and edited its manuscript version for the Cornell Yeats series.

Yeats's play survives the critics and will continue to do so. Its vigor comes from Yeats's willingness to dramatize the lower

---

65. *A Reader's Guide to the Plays of W. B. Yeats* (New York: St. Martin's Press, 1984).

66. L. A. G. Strong, reviewing the first edition of the play, mentioned that he knew what Yeats was alluding to, but coyly preferred not to explain the allusion, for reasons best known to himself. See "A Violent Fable" in *The Spectator* 160, no. 5722 (February 25, 1938), 330.

67. "Prosecutors Will Be Violated: Sexuality and Heroism in *The Herne's Egg*," *Canadian Journal of Irish Studies* 11, no. 2 (December 1983), 43–56.

## INTRODUCTION

depths of human nature together with its spiritual aspirations and to see them both with irony, for the mere existence of each throws an ironic light on the other. Its vigor also comes from the theatrical energy of its unearthly song, the choreographed battle and stoning of the god, Attracta's mediumistic behavior and her dance: these elements make for vivid, arresting effects in performance. They forcefully suggest also the presence of a god, one that is missed by critics who fail to read the text for its potential in the theater. That is something we ignore at our peril.

## NOTE ON THE TEXT

Yeats revised his previously finished plays for publication in *The Collected Plays of W. B. Yeats* (1934). *The Herne's Egg*, written later, was first published by Macmillan of London in 1938. In the same year it appeared in *The Herne's Egg and Other Plays* with a brief Preface by Yeats from Macmillan in New York. After his death, it was included with the other post-1934 plays, *A Full Moon in March, The King of the Great Clock Tower, Purgatory,* and *The Death of Cuchulain,* in *The Collected Plays of W. B. Yeats* (1952). Russell K. Alspach used this as the base text for his essential *Variorum Edition of the Plays of W. B. Yeats* (1965). Paperback selections of Yeats's plays edited by A. N. Jeffares follow the 1952 text. The relation of the present edition to the previous versions of the play may be represented diagrammatically as shown.

The 1952 version of *The Herne's Egg* differs in a number of ways from the first edition of 1938. First, there were changes in format: *1938*'s conventions for stage directions were simple and consistent. All directions were in italics and unbracketed except for a number of, but not all the *brief* directions indicating a stage effect or stage business during a scene, e.g., "(*Throws a table-leg on the floor.*)" *1952* and *Variorum* have all directions in italics, with those at the beginning of the scene unbracketed; scene 2 then establishes the convention of opening but not closing square brackets around directions occurring within the scene. This is true of the exits and entrances. In scene 4 the convention of the bracket is silently dropped for Congal's entry *solus* and later with his men. The same convention is silently dropped in scenes 5 and 6 for entries but retained in scene 6 for exits. None of these accidentals introduced in *1952* or *Variorum* seems to me superior to those of *1938*; I have preferred the simpler conventions of the first edition but with square brackets around all in-scene directions.

Secondly, *1952* introduced a few changes in punctuation to improve the earlier text in minor ways. These changes I have

|                              | Prose Scenario (December 1935) |                              |
| (Autograph?)                 | (Lost?)                        |                              |
|                              |                                |                              |
| (Autograph)                  | Verse Drafts (December 1935 and later) |                      |
|                              | (Lost?)                        |                              |
|                              |                                |                              |
| (Autograph; not a fair copy) | *MS 8770* (1), (2) (National Library of Ireland) | |
|                              | Fair Copy?                     |                              |
|                              |                                |                              |
|                              ┌── Typescript                   |                              |
| (Submitted to Macmillan. Carbon copy later sent to Scribner?) | (Lost?) | |
|                              | Proof Sheets                   |                              |
|                              | (Lost?)                        |                              |
|                              | *The Herne's Egg* (London, 1938) |                            |
|                              |                                | *The Herne's Egg and Other Plays* (New York, 1938) (Brief Preface) |
| Yeats's amended copy of *1938* |                              |                              |
| └── Scribner's TS            |                                |                              |
| (Amended carbon)             |                                |                              |
| Two sheets of amendments. (These and *Scribner's TS* in Harry Ransom Humanities Research Center, the University of Texas at Austin) | | |
| *Collected Plays* (London, 1952) |                            | *Collected Plays* (New York, 1953) |
| *Eleven Plays* (ed. Jeffares) (New York, 1964) (London, 1964) | | |
| *Variorum Plays* (ed. Alspach) (London, 1965) | | |
|                              | Present Edition                |                              |

# NOTE ON THE TEXT

noted, and altered the *1938* punctuation where improvement resulted. I have changed commas to parentheses in the cast list; the position of speakers' names follows the convention of the series.

Thirdly, there were substantive variants that deserve mention: in *Scribner's TS* and *1938* the full moon of the final scene is described in the opening stage directions as about to rise but is not seen by the audience until it rises at the very moment when Congal strikes himself a fatal blow. *1952* sacrifices this effect in favor of having the moon already risen at the beginning of the scene. It also supplies extra lines for Corney, Congal, and Attracta. No authority is given for these or other additions either in *1952* or *Variorum*, though Edward O'Shea's *Descriptive Catalog* lists the additions as marginalia in Yeats's hand on the poet's own copy of the play's 1938 English edition. These additions most likely originated when Yeats was preparing for Charles Scribner's a Collected Poetry and Prose. The extant *Scribner's TS* has the alterations written on it, some in ink in Yeats's hand, some in pencil by BS, an employee at Scribner's. This TS is a carbon copy, probably of the top copy TS used to prepare *1938*. The carbon copy TS was accompanied by two top copy sheets listing the desired alterations. The Scribner's collection was abandoned. The 1938 American edition is identical to the English first edition, except that it drops the question mark from Agnes's unfinished line "When he comes—will he?—." All other texts retain this question mark.

My procedure has been to use as copy-text the first English edition, *1938,* since this appeared during Yeats's lifetime and he corrected its proofs. Furthermore, the *1952* additions do not resolve the problems with the number of soldiers or Kate's eggs (see Introduction). Nor are they always improvements. They can be considered in general as speculative afterthoughts, not having the authority of post-production thinking and revision. They were, however, printed while Mrs. Yeats was still alive, and are not to be lightly disregarded. I give them therefore as notes rather than incorporate them into the text of the play Yeats himself published.

For detail on the editions of *The Herne's Egg* see:

Russell K. Alspach, *The Variorum Edition of the Plays of W. B. Yeats* (London: Macmillan, 1966).
Allen Wade, *A Bibliography of the Writings of W. B. Yeats* (London: Rupert Hart-Davis, 1951; 1958 and 1968 rev.).
Edward O'Shea, *A Descriptive Catalog of W. B. Yeats's Library* (New York and London: Garland, 1985).

# CRITICAL BIBLIOGRAPHY

Works listed here are those most frequently consulted or referred to in preparing this edition. For the most complete listing of critical material to 1972 see: K. P. S. Jochum, *W. B. Yeats: A Classified Bibliography of Criticism* (Urbana: Univ. of Illinois Press; London: Dawson, 1978). For later criticism see *Yeats: An Annual of Critical and Textual Studies,* Vols. 1–3, ed. R. J. Finneran (Ithaca and London: Cornell Univ. Press, 1983–85) and *Yeats Annual,* Vols. 3–5, ed. W. Gould (London: Macmillan; Atlantic Highlands, N.J.: Humanities Press, 1985–86, continuing).

Alspach, Russell K., ed. *Variorum Edition of the Plays of W. B. Yeats.* London: Macmillan, 1966.
Archibald, Douglas. *Yeats.* Syracuse: Syracuse University Press, 1983.
Bloom, Harold. *Yeats.* New York: Oxford University Press, 1970.
Clark, David R. *W. B. Yeats and the Theatre of Desolate Reality.* Dublin: Dolmen, 1965.
Ellis-Fermor, Una. *The Irish Dramatic Movement.* London: Methuen, 1954 rev.
Ellmann, Richard. *Yeats: The Man and the Masks.* London: Macmillan, 1961. First published London: Faber, 1949.
———. *The Identity of Yeats.* London: Macmillan, 1954.
Fenollosa, Ernest, and Ezra Pound (trans. and ed.). *"Noh" or Accomplishment: A Study of the Classical Stage of Japan.* New York: New Directions, 1959.
Ferguson, Sir Samuel. *Congal, A Poem in Five Books.* Dublin: Ponsonby, 1872.
Flannery, James W. *W. B. Yeats and the Idea of a Theatre.* New Haven: Yale University Press, 1977.
Gregory, Lady Augusta. *Our Irish Theatre.* Gerrards Cross, Bucks: Colin Smythe, 1972. First published New York and London: Putnam, 1913.

Harper, George Mills. *The Mingling of Heaven and Earth: Yeats's Theory of Theatre.* Dublin: Dolmen, 1975.
Hone, Joseph. *W. B. Yeats, 1865–1939.* London: Macmillan; New York: St. Martin's Press, 1962 rev.
Hough, Graham. *The Mystery Religion of W. B. Yeats.* London: Harvester Press; Totowa, NJ: Barnes and Noble, 1984.
Jeffares, A. Norman. *W. B. Yeats: Man and Poet.* London: Routledge & Kegan Paul, 1962 rev. First published, 1949.
Jeffares, A. Norman, and A. S. Knowland. *A Commentary on the Collected Plays of W. B. Yeats.* London: Macmillan, 1975.
Krimm, Bernard G. *W. B. Yeats and the Emergence of the Irish Free State.* Troy, NY: Whitston Publishing Co., 1981.
Maxwell, D. E. S. *Modern Irish Drama, 1891–1980.* Cambridge: Cambridge University Press, 1984.
Melchiori, Giorgio. *The Whole Mystery of Art: Pattern into Poetry in the Work of W. B. Yeats.* London: Routledge & Kegan Paul, 1960.
Moore, John Rees. *Masks of Love and Death: Yeats as Dramatist.* New York and London: Columbia University Press, 1965.
Nathan, Leonard E. *The Tragic Drama of William Butler Yeats.* New York and London: Columbia University Press, 1965.
O'Driscoll, Robert, and Lorna Reynolds, eds. *Yeats and the Theatre.* Toronto: Macmillan of Canada, 1975.
Saul, George Brandon. *Prolegomena to the Study of Yeats's Plays.* Philadelphia: University of Pennsylvania Press, 1958.
Taylor, Richard. *A Reader's Guide to the Plays of W. B. Yeats.* New York: St. Martin's Press, 1984.
Ure, Peter. *Yeats the Playwright.* London: Routledge & Kegan Paul, 1963.
Vendler, Helen. *Yeats's Vision and the Later Plays.* Cambridge: Harvard University Press, 1963.
Wade, Allan. *The Letters of W. B. Yeats.* London: Rupert Hart-Davis, 1954.
Webster, Brenda S. *Yeats: A Psychoanalytic Study.* Stanford: Stanford University Press, 1973.
Whitaker, Thomas. *Swan and Shadow: Yeats's Dialogue with History.* Chapel Hill: University of North Carolina Press, 1964. Washington, DC: The Catholic University of America Press, 1989.
Wilson, F. A. C. *W. B. Yeats and Tradition.* London: Victor Gollancz, 1958.

———. *Yeats's Iconography.* London: Gollancz, 1961.
Worth, Katharine. *The Irish Drama of Europe from Yeats to Beckett.* Atlantic Highlands, NJ: Humanities Press, 1978.
Yeats, W. B. *A Vision.* New York: Macmillan, 1961.
———. *Essays and Introductions.* New York: Macmillan, 1961.
———. *Explorations.* New York: Macmillan, 1962.

# THE HERNE'S EGG

# PERSONS[1]

CONGAL[2]  *(King of Connaught)*[3]
AEDH[4]  *(King of Tara)*[5]
CORNEY  *(Attracta's servant)*
MIKE, PAT, MALACHI, MATHIAS, PETER,
   JOHN  *(Connaught soldiers)*[6]
ATTRACTA  *(A Priestess)*
KATE, AGNES, MARY  *(Friends of Attracta)*
Soldiers of Tara
A FOOL[7]

---

   1. "Persons" Main characters not given in order of appearance on stage in *1952*, but listed in two columns.
   2. "Congal" An Ulster king, defeated and slain in A.D. 637 at the battle of Moyra, when organized druidism was dealt a death blow, ensuring the dominance of Christianity.
   3. "Connaught" *1952*: "Connacht," a change in spelling made consistently.
   4. "Aedh" A king (A.D. 566–93) who fell in battle at Dunbold. In Ferguson's poem it was Aedh's son who fought Congal.
   5. "Tara" Hill in Co. Meath, seat of high kings of Ireland. Since Tara is in Eastern Ireland and Connacht in the West, Yeats, by making his combatants kings of these regions, sets up a conflict between East and West that could be interpreted on political, religious, and philosophical levels.
   6. "Connaught soldiers" The soldier James is not listed in any edition. Congal and his men come from the last stronghold of the "wild Irish."
   7. "Soldiers . . . Fool" *1952* reverses order.

# SCENE I

*Mist and rocks; high up on backcloth a rock, its base hidden in mist; on this rock stands a great herne. All should be suggested, not painted realistically.*[8] *Many men fighting with swords and shields, but sword and sword, shield and sword, never meet. The men move rhythmically as if in a dance; when swords approach one another cymbals clash; when swords and shields approach drums boom. The battle flows out at one side; two Kings are left fighting in the centre of the stage; the battle returns and flows out at the other side.*[9] *The two Kings remain, but are now face to face and motionless. They are Congal, King of Connaught, and Aedh, King of Tara.*

| | |
|---|---|
| CONGAL | How many men have you lost? |
| AEDH | Some five-and-twenty men. |
| CONGAL | No need to ask my losses. |
| AEDH | Your losses equal mine. |
| CONGAL | They always have and must. |
| AEDH | Skill, strength, arms matched. |
| CONGAL | Where is the wound this time? |
| AEDH | There, left shoulder-blade. |

   8. The stage directions show Yeats's preference for nonrealistic, stylized sets for his verse plays. The description of the backcloth is specific, and Yeats's knowledge of Japanese art is relevant.
   9. "The battle" recalls the choreographed action of the dance version of *The Only Jealousy of Emer*, published as *Fighting the Waves*.

| | |
|---|---|
| CONGAL | Here, right shoulder-blade. |
| AEDH | Yet we have fought all day. |
| CONGAL | This is our fiftieth battle.[10] |
| AEDH | And all were perfect battles. |
| CONGAL | Come, sit upon this stone.<br>Come and take breath awhile. |
| AEDH | From day-break[11] until noon,<br>Hopping among these rocks. |
| CONGAL | Nothing to eat or drink. |
| AEDH | A story is running round<br>Concerning two rich fleas. |
| CONGAL | We hop like fleas, but war<br>Has taken all our riches. |
| AEDH | Rich, and rich, so rich that they<br>Retired and bought a dog. |
| CONGAL | Finish the tale and say<br>What kind of dog they bought. |
| AEDH | Heaven knows. |
| CONGAL | You must have thought<br>What kind of dog they bought. |
| AEDH | Heaven knows. |
| CONGAL | Unless you say,<br>I'll up and fight all day. |

    10. "fiftieth battle" *MS8770*: hundredth (Yeats also gives casualties as 400 or 500).

    11. "day-break" *1952* "daybreak." Hyphenation used in *1938* was already archaic. A chain of rhymes on "day," "bought," and "knows" increases the symmetry of this dialogue.

| AEDH | A fat, square, lazy dog, |
| | No sort of scratching dog. |

## SCENE II

*The same place as in previous scene. Corney enters, leading a donkey,*[12] *a donkey on wheels like a child's toy, but life-size.*

| CORNEY | A tough, rough mane, a tougher skin, |
| | Strong legs though somewhat thin, |
| | A strong body, a level line |
| | Up to the neck along the spine. |
| | All good points, and all are spoilt |
| | By that rapscallion Clareman's[13] eye! |
| | What if before your present shape |
| | You could slit purses and break hearts, |
| | You are a donkey now, a chattel, |
| | A taker of blows, not a giver of blows. |
| | No tricks, you're not in County Clare, |
| | No, not one kick upon the shin. |

[*Congal, Pat, Mike, James, Mathias, Peter, John, enter,*[14] *in the dress and arms of the previous scene but without shields.*]

| CONGAL | I have learned of a great hernery |
| | Among these rocks, and that a woman, |
| | Prophetess or priestess, named Attracta, |
| | Owns it—take this donkey and man, |
| | Look for the creels, pack them with eggs. |

| MIKE | Manners! |

---

    12. a donkey *1952*: "Donkey, a donkey, . . ." Though using lowercase here, *1938* adopts capital in subsequent stage directions.

    13. "rapscallion Clareman" An anachronism since County Clare before 1580 was called Tuadmumu. Yeats used the modern name perhaps because it was well known as de Valera's constituency. The satire could thus be general and specific. In *Scribner's TS* the county was Mayo and the speech two lines longer.

    14. "Congal, Pat, Mike, James, Mathias, Peter, John, enter" Stage directions of all texts here omit Malachi and include James, who is missing from the list of Persons, p. 40. This establishes seven soldiers, but the audience would not be aware of the substitution, since dialogue has not named them. Since Yeats later writes dialogue for both Malachi and James, we can perhaps assume he had merely confused these two.

CONGAL  This man is in the right.
I will ask Attracta for the eggs
If you will tell how to summon her.

CORNEY  A flute[15] lies there upon the rock
Carved out of a herne's thigh.
Go pick it up and play the tune
My mother[16] calls 'The Great Herne's Feather'.
If she has a mind to come, she will come.

CONGAL  That's a queer way of summoning.

CORNEY  This is a holy place and queer;
But if you do not know that tune,
Custom permits that I should play it,
But you must cross my hand with silver.

[*Congal gives money, and Corney plays flute.*]

CONGAL  Go pack the donkey creels with eggs.

[*All go out except Congal and Mike. Attracta enters.*]

ATTRACTA  For a thousand or ten thousand years,
For who can count so many years,
Some woman has lived among these rocks,
The Great Herne's bride, or promised bride,
And when a visitor has played the flute
Has come or not.[17] What would you ask?

CONGAL  Tara and I have made a peace;
Our fiftieth battle fought,[18] there is need

---

15. "flute" Cf. the First Musician's song in *Calvary*: "As though a flute of bone / Taken from a heron's thigh, / A heron crazed by the moon, / Were cleverly, softly played." Both plays associate the somewhat sinister image with a subjective god. Unlike the First Musician of the earlier play, Congal is not afraid.

16. mother *MS8770*: "Mother," suggesting he refers to the Great Mother or Earth Goddess. In view of his next line, his "mother" could in a symbolic (though not natural) sense be Attracta, priestess of the region, who on one level is a type of *the* mother, or Virgin Mother Goddess.

17. "Has come or not" Attracta suggests the tune does not automatically summon her. Congal failed in fact to play the tune. Presumably she appears to those travelers whom the Great Herne decides to use in some way.

18. "Our fiftieth battle fought" See note 10. The number is small compared

## SCENE II

|   |   |
|---|---|
| | Of preparation for the next;
He and all his principal men,
I and all my principal men,
Take supper at his principal house
This night, in his principal city, Tara,
And we have set our minds upon
A certain novelty or relish. |
| MIKE | Herne's eggs. |
| CONGAL | This man declares our need;
A donkey, both creels packed with eggs,
Somebody that knows the mind of a donkey
For donkey-boy. |
| ATTRACTA | Custom forbids:
Only the women of these rocks,
Betrothed or married to the Herne,
The god or ancestor of hernes,
Can eat, handle, or look upon those eggs. |
| CONGAL | Refused! Must old campaigners lack
The one sole dish that takes their fancy,
My cooks what might have proved their skill,
Because a woman thinks that she
Is promised or married to a bird? |
| MIKE | Mad! |
| CONGAL | Mad! This man is right,
But you are not to blame for that.
Women thrown into despair[19]
By the winter of their virginity
Take its abominable snow,
As boys take common snow, and make |

---

with Attracta's time frame of thousands of years. This effect contrasts the short span of the human with the divine.

19. "Women thrown into despair" Cf. "For Anne Gregory." The speech links Attracta with the Queen of *The Player Queen* and the cruel Queen of *A Full Moon in March*. Melchiori (*WMA*, 196–97) points to Mallarmé's "Hérodiade" translated by Symons as Yeats's source. See W. B. Yeats, *Autobiographies* (London: Macmillan, 1955; rep. 1956), p. 321.

> An image of god or bird or beast
> To feed their sensuality:
> Ovid had a literal mind,[20]
> And though he sang it neither knew
> What lonely lust[21] dragged down the gold
> That crept on Danae's lap, nor knew
> What rose against the moony feathers
> When Leda lay upon the grass.

ATTRACTA   There is no reality but the Great Herne.

MIKE   The cure.

CONGAL   Why, that is easy said;
> An old campaigner is the cure
> For everything that woman dreams—
> Even I myself, had I but time.

MIKE   Seven men.[22]

CONGAL   This man of learning means
> That seven men packed into a day
> Or dawdled out through seven years
> And not a weather-stained, war-battered
> Old campaigner such as I,[23]
> Are needed to melt down the snow
> That's fallen among these wintry rocks.

ATTRACTA   There is no happiness but the Great Herne.

   20. Congal's proposed cure for Attracta recalls Ovid's *Remedia Amoris*. Considering his fate in the play, it is an irony against Congal that he disparages the author of *Metamorphoses*.
   21. "What lonely lust" The last four lines of the speech assume women really desire rape. But Danae and Leda were both quite clearly innocent victims; in neither case do the basic myths suggest the complicity of the women. For sources of Yeats's poem on the subject see Ian Fletcher, "'Leda and the Swan' as Iconic Poem" in *Yeats Annual*, no. 1 (1982), 82–113.
   22. "Seven men" Mike suggests seven *other* than Congal, who has said he is too busy.
   23. "Seven years . . . as I" *1952*: "Years— . . . as I,—." The punctuation added in *1952* results in the ugly comma and dash after *I*. The addition of a comma after *years* is preferable to dashes. Nor is the reordering of lines necessary. *1952* has ". . . not a weather-stained, war-battered / Old campaigner such as I,—" to follow "That . . . ," continuing with "But seven men packed into a day / Or dawdled out through seven years— / Are needed. . . ."

## SCENE II

CONGAL  It may be that life is suffering,
But youth that has not yet known pleasure
Has not the right to say so; pick,
Or be picked by seven men,
And we shall talk it out again.[24]

ATTRACTA  Being betrothed to the Great Herne
I know what may be known: I burn
Not in the flesh but in the mind;
Chosen out of all my kind
That I may lie in a blazing bed
And a bird take my maidenhead,
To the unbegotten I return,
All a womb and a funeral urn.

[*Enter Corney, Pat, James, Mathias, etc., with Donkey. A creel packed with eggs is painted upon the side of the Donkey.*]

CORNEY  Think of yourself; think of the songs:
Bride of the Herne, and the Great Herne's bride,
Grow terrible: go into a trance.

ATTRACTA  Stop!

CORNEY  Bring the god out of your gut;[25]
Stand there asleep until the rascals
Wriggle upon his beak like eels.

ATTRACTA  Stop!

CORNEY  The country calls them rascals,
I, sacrilegious rascals that have taken
Every new-laid egg in the hernery.

ATTRACTA  Stop! When have I permitted you
To say what I may, or may not do?
But you and your donkey must obey
All big men who can say their say.

---

24. "men . . . again" Congal's couplet prepared for Attracta's fully rhymed speech that follows.

25. "Bring the god out of your gut" Corney, believing in Attracta's powers, yearns for crude miracle.

CONGAL    And bid him keep a civil tongue.

ATTRACTA  Those eggs are stolen from the god.
          It is but right that you hear said
          A curse so ancient that no man
          Can say who made it,²⁶ any thing at all
          But that it was nailed upon a post
          And has not failed these thousand years.
          Maybe it was the Great Herne who made it.²⁷

CORNEY    Hernes must stand on one leg when they fish
          In honour of the bird who made it.

          "This they nailed upon a post
          On the night my leg was lost,"
          *Said the old, old herne that had but one leg.*

          "He that a herne's egg dare steal
          Shall be changed into a fool,"
          *Said the old, old herne that had but one leg.*

          "And to end his fool breath
          At a fool's hand meet his death,"
          *Said the old, old herne that had but one leg.*²⁸

CONGAL    That I shall live and die a fool,
          And die upon some battlefield²⁹
          At some fool's hand, is but natural,
          And needs no curse to bring it.

26. "Can say who made it," *1952*: "Can say who made it, or anything at all / But that it was nailed upon a post / Before a herne had stood on one leg." The addition of "or" clarifies the sense but destroys the pentameter. The deletion of Attracta's last two lines in *1952* suppresses the uncertainty suggested by *maybe*.

27. "And has . . . made it" Omitted in *1952*.

28. *1952* uses single quotation marks in the curse, after which Corney has the following lines: "I think it was the Great Herne made it, / Pretending that he had but the one leg / To fool us all; but Great Herne or another / It has not failed these thousand years." But *Scribner's TS*, a source for *1952*, reads "Leg / To fool them all." The reattribution of Attracta's last two lines adds to Corney's characterisation, giving him uncertainty in the first and certainty in the last line here.

29. "And die upon some battlefield" Jeffares notes (*Com. Pl.*, 270) this is Congal's idea and not in the curse. *MS 8770* makes no mention of death on the battlefield at this point. The idea was a later addition rather than early dialogue inadvertently left in the play.

## SCENE II

MIKE                    Pickled!

CONGAL     He says that I am an old campaigner
           Robber of sheepfolds and cattle trucks,
           So, cursed from morning until midnight,
           There is not a quarter of an inch
           To plaster a new curse on.[30]

CORNEY                  Luck![31]

CONGAL     Adds that your luck begins when you
           Recall that though we took those eggs
           We paid with good advice; and then
           Take to your bosom seven men.

[*Congal, Mike, Corney, Mathias, James, and Donkey go out.*[32] *Enter timidly three girls, Kate, Agnes, Mary.*]

MARY       Have all those fierce men gone?

ATTRACTA   All those fierce men have gone.

AGNES      But they will come again?

ATTRACTA   No, never again.

KATE       We bring three presents.

[*All except Attracta kneel.*]

MARY       This is a jug of cream.

AGNES      This is a bowl of butter.

    30. "So . . . midnight, . . . on." *1952*: "So . . . midnight . . . upon." The addition of the final syllable in *1952* overlooks the fact that "Luck!", which follows, actually completes the four beat line in *1938*.
    31. "Luck!" All editions attribute this to Corney, though it is more properly attributed to Mike, since Congal's "Adds that . . ." refers to his previous interpretation of Mike's last line. Congal thinks Mike, not Corney, has spoken. *Scribner's TS*: "Wriggling rascals!" *1938* thus changed a remark appropriate for Corney into one appropriate for Mike.
    32. "Congal . . . Donkey go out" Yeats does not remove John, Peter, and Pat here. Since nothing develops from their presence, we may assume Yeats forgot them; he had earlier forgotten to bring in Malachi, using James instead.

KATE    This is a basket of eggs.

[*They lay jug, bowl, and basket on the ground.*]

ATTRACTA    I know what you would ask.
Sit round upon these stones.
Children, why do you fear
A woman but little older,
A child yesterday?
All, when I am married,
Shall have good husbands. Kate
Shall marry a black-headed lad.

AGNES    She swore but yesterday
That she would marry black.

ATTRACTA    But Agnes there shall marry
A honey-coloured lad.

AGNES    O!

ATTRACTA    Mary shall be married
When I myself am married
To the lad that is in her mind.

MARY    Are you not married yet?

ATTRACTA    No. But it is almost come,
May come this very night.

MARY    And must he be all feathers?

AGNES    Have a terrible beak?

KATE    Great terrible claws?

ATTRACTA    Whatever shape he choose,
Though that be terrible,
Will best express his love.

─────── SCENE II ───────

AGNES        When he comes—will he?—³³

ATTRACTA     Child, ask what you please.

AGNES        Do all that a man does?

ATTRACTA     Strong sinew and soft flesh
             Are foliage round the shaft
             Before the arrowsmith
             Has stripped it, and I pray
             That I, all foliage gone,
             May shoot into my joy—³⁴

[*Sound of a flute, playing 'The Great Herne's Feather'.*]

MARY         Who plays upon that flute?

AGNES        Her god is calling her.

KATE         Look, look, she takes
             An egg out of the basket.
             My white hen laid it,
             My favourite white hen.

MARY         Her eyes grow glassy, she moves
             According to the notes of the flute.

AGNES        Her limbs grow rigid, she seems
             A doll upon a wire.

MARY         Her human life is gone
             And that is why she seems
             A doll upon a wire.

    33. "Will he?—" *Collected Plays* (New York, 1953) omits question mark. *Variorum* misses this accidental, though noting all other variants in that edition.
    34. "Strong sinew . . . my joy" Cf. Yeats's version of part of the Katha-Upanishad: "Man should strip him of the body as the arrow-maker strips the reed, that he may know God as perpetual and pure" (*The Ten Principal Upanishads*). Yeats earlier employed the image of the arrow streaking heavenward in "The Phases of the Moon." Yet in the context of the discussion about her wedding night Attracta's imagery is irresistibly sexual, reflecting ambiguities in the play's central situation as well as in this specific scene, where Attracta, little more than a girl like the others, is also a sacred bride.

| | |
|---|---|
| AGNES | You mean that when she looks so<br>She is but a puppet? |
| MARY | How do I know? And yet<br>Twice have I seen her so,<br>She will move for certain minutes<br>As though her god were there<br>Thinking how best to move<br>A doll upon a wire.<br>Then she will move away<br>In long leaps as though<br>He had remembered his skill.<br>She has still my little egg.[35] |
| AGNES | Who knows but your little egg<br>Comes into some mystery? |
| KATE | Some mystery to make<br>Love-loneliness more sweet. |
| AGNES | She has moved. She has moved away. |
| KATE | Travelling fast asleep<br>In long loops like a dancer. |
| MARY | Like a dancer, like a hare. |
| AGNES | The last time she went away<br>The moon was full[36]—she returned<br>Before its side had flattened. |
| KATE | This time she will not return. |

---

35. "She has still my little egg" In *MS 8770* (1) this is Mary's reply to Jane's speech about the bridal torch; to arrive at our text, Yeats changed Jane to Kate and expanded Mary's role to stress her affinities with the Virgin Mary. Kate, not Mary, brought in the eggs.

36. "The moon was full" In Yeats's system, the full moon is at phase fifteen (of its twenty-eight phase cycle) representing total subjectivity, attainable by spiritual beings though not by living humanity. The full moon would be an appropriate time for the mystic marriage to a subjective divinity.

─────────── SCENE II ───────────

AGNES  Because she is called to her marriage?

KATE  Those leaps may carry her where
No woman has gone, and he
Extinguish sun, moon, star.
No bridal torch can burn
When his black midnight is there.[37]

AGNES  I have heard her claim that they couple
In the blazing heart of the sun.

KATE  But you have heard it wrong!
In blue-black midnight they couple.

AGNES  No, in the sun.

KATE  Blue-black![38]

AGNES  In the sun!

KATE  Blue-black, blue-black!

MARY  All I know is that she
Shall lie there in his bed,
Nor shall it end until
She lies there full of his might,[39]
His thunderbolts in her hand.

---

37. "Extinguish sun, . . . there" The utter darkness Kate imagines for Attracta's bridal night recalls the notion that "Where there is Nothing there is God" which Yeats had explored in his earlier play of that title. He also associates darkness with the emergence of a god in the opening and closing songs of *The Resurrection*.

38. "No, in the sun. Blue-black!" The quarrel as to when Attracta couples with the Great Herne is really a quarrel about whether the Herne is a primary (sun) or antithetical (moon) divinity. Her night-time rape suggests, insofar as it represents her sacred marriage to the Herne, that Attracta and the Herne represent antithetical or subjective forces.

39. "bed, / Nor . . . might," *1938*: bed, / Nor . . . might" *1952*: "bed, / Nor . . . might."

## SCENE III

*Before the gates of Tara, Congal, Mike, Pat, Peter, James, Mathias, etc., soldiers of Congal,*[40] *Corney, and the Donkey.*

CONGAL  This is Tara; in a moment
Men must come out of the gate
With a great basket between them
And we give up our arms;[41]
No armed man can enter.

CORNEY  And here is that great bird
Over our heads again.

PAT  The Great Herne himself
And he in a red rage.

MIKE  Stones.

CONGAL  This man is right.[42]
Beat him to death with stones.

[*All go through the motion of picking up and throwing stones. There are no stones except in so far as their gestures can suggest them.*]

PAT  All our stones[43] fell wide.

CORNEY  He has come down so low
His legs are sweeping the grass.

MIKE  Swords.

---

40. "Before the gates . . . Congal" Yeats's stage directions do not mention the entry of Malachi or John among Congal's other soldiers. This could be to allow them to double as the two men who enter with the basket to collect the weapons, but two of Aedh's soldiers would be the logical choice for the job. Yeats's use of "etc." to end the incomplete list of Congal's soldiers in the stage directions again prevents a reader from noticing that there would be seven rather than six named men in Congal's party. The gates recall those of *The King's Threshold* (1904), adding to Yeats's element of self-parody.

41. "arms;" as *1952 1938*: "arms,"

42. "This man is right." *Scribner's TS* retains this line, following it with "The great herne cursed us all," suggesting an oversight, or that the intended Scribner's edition might have included it.

43. "All our stones" *1952*: "All those stones"

―――――――― SCENE IV ――――――――

CONGAL          This man is right.
                Cut him up with swords.

PAT             I have him within my reach.

CONGAL          No, no, he is here at my side.

CORNEY          His wing has touched my shoulder.

CONGAL          We missed him again and he
                Rises again and sinks
                Behind the wall of Tara.

[*Two men come in carrying a large basket slung between two poles. One is whistling. All except Corney, who is unarmed, drop their swords and helmets into the basket. Each soldier when he takes off his helmet shows that he wears a skull-cap of soft cloth.*]

CONGAL          Where have I heard that tune?

MIKE            This morning.

CONGAL                  I know it now,
                The tune of 'The Great Herne's Feather'.
                It puts my teeth on edge.

### SCENE IV

*Banqueting hall. A throne painted on the back-cloth.*[44] *Enter Congal, alone, drunk, and shouting.*

CONGAL          To arms, to arms! Connaught to arms!
                Insulted and betrayed, betrayed and insulted.
                Who has insulted me? Tara has insulted.
                To arms, to arms! Connaught to arms!
                To arms—but if you have not got any
                Take a table-leg or a candlestick,
                A boot or a stool or any odd thing.
                Who has betrayed me? Tara has betrayed!
                To arms, to arms! Connaught to arms!

---

44. "back-cloth" *1952*: "backcloth"

[*He goes out to one side. Music, perhaps drum and concertina, to suggest breaking of wood. Enter at the other side, the King of Tara, drunk.*]

AEDH    Where is that beastly drunken liar
That says I have insulted him?

[*Congal enters with two table-legs.*]

CONGAL    I say it!

AEDH    What insult?

CONGAL    How dare you ask?
When I have had a common egg,
A common hen's egg put before me,
An egg dropped in the dirty straw
And crowed for by a cross-bred gangling cock,[45]
And every other man at the table
A herne's egg.

[*Throws a table-leg on the floor.*]

There is your weapon. Take it!
Take it up, defend yourself.
An egg that some half-witted slattern[46]
Spat upon and wiped on her apron!

AEDH    A servant put the wrong egg there.

CONGAL    But at whose orders?

AEDH    At your own.
A murderous drunken plot, a plot
To put a weapon that I do not know
Into my hands.

    45. "gangling cock" A symbol of objectivity; cf. the cocks in two songs in *The Dreaming of the Bones* (1919). Since Congal is an objective, or primary personality, a common hen's egg is suitable for him, although he desires its opposite.
    46. "some half-witted slattern" In Ferguson's *Congal* the insult arises from the error of a kitchen hand. Congal suspects an intended insult, though his host, as here, denies it. In Yeats's play we assume the herne intends to anger Congal, since Attracta switches the eggs while in a trance, unless we take a sceptical view of the herne as god and attribute Attracta's state of mind to mere delusion.

─────────────────── SCENE IV ───────────────────

CONGAL             Take up that weapon.
            If I am as drunken as you say,
            And you as sober as you think,
            A coward and a drunkard are well matched.

[*Aedh takes up the table-leg. Connaught and Tara soldiers come in, they fight, and the fight sways to and fro. The weapons, table-legs, candlesticks, etc., do not touch. Drum-taps represent blows.*⁴⁷ *All go out fighting. Enter Pat, drunk, with bottle.*]

PAT         Herne's egg, hen's egg, great difference.⁴⁸
            There's insult in that difference.
            What do hens eat? Hens live upon mash,
            Upon slop, upon kitchen odds and ends.
            What do hernes eat? Hernes live on eels,
            On things that must always run about.
            Man's a high animal and runs about,
            But mash is low, O, very low.
            Or, to speak like a philosopher,
            When a man expects the movable
            But gets the immovable, he is insulted.⁴⁹

[*Enter Congal, Peter, Malachi, Mathias, etc.*]⁵⁰

CONGAL      Tara knew that he was overmatched;
            Knew from the start he had no chance;
            Died of a broken head; died drunk;
            Accused me with his dying breath
            Of secretly practising with a table-leg,

---

47. "Drum-taps represent blows" The drunken brawl clearly parodies the gentlemanly battle of scene 1, though it is also stylized (but see Jeffares, *Com. Pl.* 271, n. 659). Where the gong of scene 1 was impressive, the drumming in the brawl is comic.

48. "Herne's egg, hen's egg, great difference" Pat's soliloquy demonstrates how truth can be seen "out of [a] drunkard's eye" (cf. "The Seven Sages"), for his distinction between Herne and common hen is a distinction between Yeatsian antinomies, subjective and objective. The trifling provocation to battle is thus as profoundly ambiguous as the other key incident in the play, the rape or sacred marriage of Attracta.

49. "When a man . . . insulted" *Scribner's TS*: "When a man . . . inspired," destroys the 1938 text's joke, again placed after the battle, as with the joke about the dog and fleas in scene 1.

50. "Enter Congal, Peter, Malachi, Mathias, etc." Malachi named here for first time in an internal stage direction, but James, not Malachi, is given important lines in the subsequent dialogue, suggesting Attracta be put to death.

|         | Practising at midnight until I
Became a perfect master with the weapon.
But that is all lies. |
|---|---|

PAT	Let all men know
He was a noble character
And I must weep at his funeral.⁵¹

CONGAL	He insulted me with a hen's egg,
Said I had practised with a table-leg,
But I have taken kingdom and throne
And that has made all level again
And I can weep at his funeral.
I would not have had him die that way
Or die at all, he should have been immortal.
Our fifty battles had made us friends.⁵²
And there are fifty more to come.
New weapons, a new leader will be found
And everything begin again.

MIKE	Much bloodier.

CONGAL	They had, we had
Forgotten what we fought about,
So fought like gentlemen, but now
Knowing the truth must fight like the beasts.⁵³
Maybe the Great Herne's curse has done it.
Why not? Answer me that; why not?

MIKE	Horror henceforth.

CONGAL	This wise man means
We fought so long like gentlemen
That we grew blind.

---

51. "Let all men . . . funeral" Pat attempts to replace the squalor of the brawl with a certain nobility. Yeats seems to be satirizing the histrionic aspects of Irish public life. The weasel's tooth (cf. "Nineteen Hundred and Nineteen") followed by public grief was a pattern observed frequently in Ireland during Yeats's lifetime.

52. "made us friends." *1952*: "made us friends;"

53. "fight like the beasts" After Mike's previous line, Congal subscribes to the weasel's-tooth view of Irish political violence.

─────────────── SCENE IV ───────────────

[*Attracta enters, walking in her sleep,*[54] *a herne's egg in her hand. She stands near the throne and holds her egg towards it for a moment.*]

MATHIAS                      Look! Look!
               She offers that egg. Who is to take it?

CONGAL      She walks with open eyes but in her sleep.

MATHIAS     I can see it all in a flash.
               She found that herne's egg on the table
               And left the hen's egg there instead.

JAMES         She brought the hen's egg on purpose
               Walking in her wicked sleep.[55]

CONGAL      And if I take that egg, she wakes,
               Completes her task, her circle;
               We all complete a task or circle,
               Want a woman, then all goes—pff.

[*He goes to take the egg.*]

MIKE           Not now.

CONGAL             This wise man says 'not now',
               There must be something to consider first.

JAMES         By changing one egg for another
               She has brought bloodshed on us all.

PAT             He was a noble character,
               And I must weep at his funeral.

JAMES         I say that she must die, I say,[56]
               According to what my mother said,

---

    54. "walking in her sleep" Attracta's entry embodies the imagery of sight and unseeing in the dialogue.

    55. "She brought . . . sleep." *Scribner's TS* gave an earlier version of these lines to Mathias, suggesting that the reattribution of them for *1938* was a result of a decision to expand James's role.

    56. "I say . . . I say," *1952*: "I say . . . / say;" The altered punctuation is no improvement because it suggests James's mother knew what Attracta had done.

All that have done what she did must die,
But, in a manner of speaking, pleasantly,
Because legally, certainly not
By beating with a table-leg.[57]

MIKE    The Great Herne's bride.

CONGAL    I had forgotten
That all she does he makes her do,
But he is god and out of reach;
Nor stone can bruise, nor a sword pierce him,
And yet through his betrothed, his bride,
I have the power to make him suffer;[58]
His curse has given me the right,
I am to play the fool and die
At a fool's hands.

MIKE    Seven men.

[*He begins to count, seeming to strike the table[59] with the table-leg, but table and table-leg must not meet, the blow is represented by the sound of the drum.*]

One, two, three, four,
Five, six, seven men.

PAT    Seven that are present in this room,
Seven that must weep at his funeral.

CONGAL    This man who struck those seven blows
Means that we seven[60] in the name of the law
Must handle, penetrate, and possess her,
And do her a great good by that action,

57. ". . . with a table-leg." *1952*: ". . . with a table leg / As though she were a mere Tara man, / Nor yet by beating with a stone / As though she were the Great Herne himself." James instigates the kangaroo court in this scene, creating a grotesque parody of the "objective" democratic system.

58. "And yet . . . suffer" Possibly alludes to Satan's motives in Milton's *Paradise Lost*. (See Jeffares *Com. Pl.* 271, n. 662).

59. "seeming to strike the table" A vivid stage representation of phallic cruelty. The harshness also involves a maudlin rhetoric about the cause of the sentence, the death of Aedh. His murderers are hypocritically blaming Attracta for his death.

60. "We seven" Congal now includes himself, making eight not seven.

## SCENE IV

                 Melting out the virgin snow,
                 And that snow image, the Great Herne;
                 For nothing less than seven men
                 Can melt that snow, but when it melts
                 She may, being free from all obsession,
                 Live as every woman should.[61]
                 I am the Court; judgement has been given.
                 I name the seven;[62] Congal of Tara,
                 Patrick, Malachi, Mike, John, James,
                 And that coarse hulk of clay, Mathias.

MATHIAS     I dare not lay a hand upon that woman.
                 The people say that she is holy
                 And carries a great devil in her gut.[63]

PAT            What mischief can a Munster devil[64]
                 Do to a man that was born in Connaught?

MALACHI     I made a promise[65] to my mother
                 When we set out on this campaign
                 To keep from women.

JOHN                         I have a wife that's jealous
                 If I but look the moon in the face.

JAMES       I am promised to an educated girl.
                 Her family are most particular,
                 What would they say—O my God!

     61. "Live as every woman should" i.e., as subservient to human sexuality, not as serving something else. Silent virgin and drunken soldiers make a fine theatrical contrast, subverting Congal's attempt to domesticate a pagan priestess.
     62. "I name the seven" MS 8770 (1), Scribner's TS and all published texts omit Peter, who, though silent in this scene, is definitely onstage, since he is specifically named in the direction for Congal's entry.
     63. "great devil in her gut" Mathias contrasts here with Corney, who in scene 2 claimed a god inhabited Attracta's "gut." This accords with the Christian versus pagan theme. See note 25.
     64. "a Munster devil" Yeats perhaps wished to link Attracta with an indigenous mythology of the Great Mother through the Munster mother goddesses Aibhill, Anu, and Aine, for whom see James P. McGarry and Edward Malins, *Place Names in the Writings of William Butler Yeats* (Gerrards Cross: Colin Smythe, 1976) 72.
     65. "promise to my mother" Reactions of Malachi, John, and James provide comic versions of the anxieties about marriage of the three girls in scene 2.

CONGAL   Whoever disobeys the Court
         Is an unmannerly, disloyal lout,
         And no good citizen.

PAT                          Here is my bottle.
         Pass it along, a long, long pull;
         Although it's round like a woman carrying,
         No unmannerly, disloyal bottle,
         An affable, most loyal bottle.

[All drink.]

MATHIAS  I first.

CONGAL          That's for the Court to say.
         A Court of Law is a blessed thing,
         Logic, Mathematics, ground in one,
         And everything out of balance accursed.[66]
         When the Court decides on a decree
         Men carry it out with dignity.
         Here where I put down my hand
         I will put a mark, then all must stand
         Over there in a level row.
         And all take off their caps and throw.
         The nearest cap shall take her first,
         The next shall take her next, so on
         Till all is in good order done.
         I need a mark and so must take
         The herne's egg, and let her wake.

[*He takes egg and lays it upon the ground. Attracta stands motionless, looking straight in front of her. She sings. The seven standing in a row throw their caps one after another.*][67]

66. "and everything out of balance accursed" Congal's lines contain ironies: fallen from the balance of scene 1, he is himself accursed and as drunken killer cannot claim any dignity. The use of couplets ironically suggests the balance Congal talks about but has now lost. The couplets hint at the power of the herne using Congal, making him rhyme: Congal thinks he has achieved law, order, control, but it is the herne who has control.

67. "The seven . . . another" The direction is unequivocal, unlike the directions for entrances and exits of the soldiers, supporting the view that Yeats's use of eight soldiers as rapists while referring always to seven was not part of the humor in the play, but merely an error.

## SCENE V

ATTRACTA   When I take a beast to my joyful breast,
Though beak and claw I must endure,
*Sang the bride of the Herne, and the Great Herne's bride,*
No lesser life, man, bird or beast,
Can make unblessed what a beast made blessed,
Can make impure what a beast made pure.

Where is he gone, where is that other,
He that shall take my maidenhead?
*Sang the bride of the Herne, and the Great Herne's bride,*
Out of the moon came my pale brother,
The blue-black midnight is my mother.
Who will turn down the sheets of the bed?

When beak and claw their work begin
Shall horror stir in the roots of my hair?[68]
*Sang the bride of the Herne and the Great Herne's bride,*
And who lie there in the cold dawn
When all that terror has come and gone?
Shall I be the woman lying there?

### SCENE V

*Before the Gate of Tara.*[69] *Corney enters with Donkey.*

CORNEY   You thought to go on sleeping though dawn was up,
Rapscallion of a beast, old highwayman.
That light in the eastern sky is dawn,
You cannot deny it; many a time
You looked upon it following your trade.
Cheer up, we shall be home before sunset.

[*Attracta comes in.*][70]

---

68. "hair?" as *1952 1938*: "hair,"
69. "Before the Gate of Tara" Cf., "gates," p. 53, though clearly these are identical settings.
70. "Attracta comes in." Omitted in *1952*.

ATTRACTA   I have packed all the uneaten or unbroken eggs
           Into the creels. Help[71] carry them
           And hang them on the donkey's back.

CORNEY    We could boil them hard and keep them in
              the larder,
           But Congal has had them all boiled soft.

ATTRACTA   Such eggs are holy. Many pure souls[72]
           Especially among the country-people
           Would shudder if herne's eggs were left
           For foul-tongued, bloody-minded men.

[Congal, Malachi, Mike, etc., enter.][73]

CONGAL    A sensible woman;[74] you gather up what's left,
           Your thoughts upon the cupboard and the larder.
           No more a herne's bride, a crazed loony
           Waiting to be trodden by a bird,[75]
           But all woman, all sensible woman.

MIKE      Manners.

CONGAL             This man who is always right
           Desires that I should add these words,
           The seven that held you in their arms last night
           Wish you good luck.

ATTRACTA                        What do you say?
           My husband came to me in the night.

CONGAL    Seven men lay with you in the night.
           Go home desiring and desirable,
           And look for a man.

   71. "creels. Help" as *1952* *1938*: "creels, help"
   72. "souls" *1952*: "souls,"
   73. "Congal, Malachi, Mike, etc., enter." *1952*: Though Malachi is specifically mentioned here, Yeats omits to include him with the "seven" who confess to having raped Attracta a few lines later.
   74. "woman;" as *1952*. *1938*: "woman," The comma of *1938* suggests oddly that she is known as a "sensible woman" and has long been one.
   75. "bride, . . . a bird," *1952*: "bride— . . . bird—"

─────────── SCENE V ───────────

ATTRACTA           The Herne is my husband.
           I lay beside him, his pure bride.

CONGAL     Pure in the embrace of seven men?

MIKE       She slept.

CONGAL             You say that though I thought,
           Because I took the egg out of her hand,
           That she awoke, she did not wake
           Until day broke upon her sleep—
           Her sleep and ours—did she wake pure?
           Seven men can answer that.

CORNEY     King though you are, I will not hear
           The bride of the Great Herne defamed—[76]
           Seven times a liar.

MIKE                   Seven men.

CONGAL     I, Congal, lay with her last night.

MATHIAS    And I, Mathias.

MIKE                   And I.

JAMES                      And I.

PETER      And I.

JOHN               And I.

PAT                And I[77] swear it;
           And not a drop of drink since dawn.

    76. "bride of the Great Herne defamed—" *1952* adds three lines here: "A king, a king but a Mayo man. / A Mayo man's lying tongue can beat / A Clare Highwayman's rapscallion eye," *Scribner's TS*: as *1952*, but with "Bride."
    77. "And I" Followed by a semicolon in all published texts, which is confusing, because Pat is not asking the others to swear. *Scribner's TS*: "And I. / And no drop . . ." Yeats probably envisaged the actor playing drunk and pausing before slurring the word "swear."

CORNEY     One plain liar, six men bribed to lie.

ATTRACTA   Great Herne, Great Herne, Great Herne,
           Your darling is crying out,
           Great Herne, declare her pure,
           Pure as that beak and claw,
           Great Herne, Great Herne, Great Herne,
           Let the round heaven declare it.

[*Silence.*[78] *Then low thunder growing louder. All except Attracta and Congal kneel.*]

JAMES      Great Herne, I swear that she is pure;
           I never laid a hand upon her.

MATHIAS    I was a fool to believe myself
           When everybody knows that I am a liar.

PAT        Even when it seemed that I covered her
           I swear that I knew it was the drink.

ATTRACTA   I lay in the bride-bed,
           His thunderbolts in my hand,[79]
           But gave them back,[80] for he,
           My lover, the Great Herne,
           Knows everything that is said
           And every man's intent,
           And every man's deed; and he
           Shall give these seven that say
           That they upon me lay
           A most memorable punishment.

[*It thunders. All prostrate themselves except Attracta and Congal. Congal had half knelt, but he has stood up again.*]

---

78. "Silence" Stage device to build suspense. Thunder, more startling after silence, confirms Attracta's sense of spiritual reality.
79. "His thunderbolts in my hand," Cf. Mary's line that ends scene 2 (p. 53). This slightly strengthens the hint that Mary will be a sacred bride.
80. "But gave them back," She thinks she shared her god's power and knowledge, answering the question at the end of "Leda and the Swan." Rather than use the god's power on the spot she leaves the herne to punish her violators, thus preparing for the compassion she will later feel for Congal.

―――――― SCENE V ――――――

ATTRACTA   I share his knowledge, and I know
                 Every punishment decreed.
                 He will come when you are dead,
                 Push you down a step or two
                 Into cat or rat or bat,
                 Into dog or wolf or goose.[81]
                 Everybody in his new shape I can see,
                 But Congal there stands in a cloud
                 Because his fate is not yet settled.
                 Speak out, Great Herne, and make it known
                 That everything I have said is true.

[*Thunder. All now, except Attracta, have prostrated themselves.*]

ATTRACTA   What has made you kneel?

CONGAL                             This man
                 That's prostrate at my side would say,
                 Could he say anything at all,
                 That I am terrified by thunder.

ATTRACTA   Why did you stand up so long?

CONGAL   I held you in my arms last night,[82]
                We seven held you in our arms.

ATTRACTA   You were under the curse, in all
                 You did, in all you seemed to do.

CONGAL   If I must die at a fool's hand,
                When must I die?

ATTRACTA                   When the moon is full.

CONGAL   And where?

    81. "Push . . . goose." Congal's men are faced (somewhat comically) with punitive transmigration of the soul.
    82. "I held you in my arms last night" Congal, still defiant, reiterates his version of the rape.

ATTRACTA    Upon the holy mountain,
Upon Slieve Fuadh,[83] there we shall meet again[84]
Just as the moon comes round the hill.
There all the gods must visit me,[85]
Acknowledging my marriage to a god;
I would have one man[86] among those gods.

CONGAL    I know the place and I will come,
Although it be my death, I will come.
Because I am terrified, I will come.

SCENE VI

*A mountain-top, the moon is about to rise;*[87] *the moon of comic tradition, a round smiling face.*[88] *A cauldron lid, a cooking-pot, and a spit*[89] *lie together at one side of the stage. The Fool,*[90] *a man in ragged clothes, enters carrying a large stone;*[91] *he lays it down at one side and goes out. Congal enters carrying a wine-skin, and stands at the other side of the stage. The fool re-enters with a second large stone which he places beside the first.*

CONGAL    What is your name, boy?

---

83. "Slieve Fuadh" Highest peak of the Fews range in County Armagh, where Conall Cornach protects the borders of Ulster in *The Táin*; also associated with Naisi and Deirdre.
84. "we shall meet again" *1952*: "we meet again"
85. "There all the gods must visit me" Attracta perhaps anticipates a mystical experience similar to that described in Yeats's essay "An Indian Monk" (*E & I*, 426–37).
86. "I would have one man" *1952*: "One man will I have," stressing Attracta's will distinct from the herne's.
87. "the moon is about to rise" *1952*: "the moon has just risen." This places the entire scene under the comic moon's influence, but destroys the special effect of *1938* later in the scene. No authority for *1952* change is given in *Scribner's TS*.
88. "a round smiling face" Yeats's mystical full moon, parodied by the moon of pantomime or music hall, is in keeping with the play's combination of farce and symbolic action.
89. "A cauldron . . . a spit" The items are a grim joke; Congal has cooked herne's eggs and now the herne is about to "cook" Congal, perhaps suggesting the ritual eating of god and hero in mythology. They are the Fool's armaments, being a parody of shield, helmet, and spear.
90. "The Fool" appeared in earlier Yeats plays, *The Hour Glass* (1903) and *On Baile's Strand* (1904). Paradoxically wise like Shakespeare's fools, Yeats's fool is derived as well from folktale and legend. Here he is an instrument of death and dressed in rags

———————— SCENE VI ————————

FOOL                                  Poor Tom Fool.
Everybody knows Tom Fool.

CONGAL     I saw something in the mist,
There lower down upon the slope,
I went up close to it and saw
A donkey, somebody's stray donkey.
A donkey and a Fool—I don't like it at all.

FOOL         I won't be Tom the Fool after to-night.
I have made a level patch out there,
Clearing away the stones, and there
I shall fight a man and kill a man
And get great glory.

CONGAL                   Where did you get
The cauldron lid, the pot and the spit?

FOOL         I sat in Widow Rooney's kitchen,[92]
Somebody said, 'King Congal's on the mountain
Cursed to die at the hands of a fool'.
Somebody else said 'Kill him, Tom'.
And everybody began to laugh
And said I should kill him at the full moon,
And that is to-night.

CONGAL                   I too have heard
That Congal is to die to-night.
Take a drink.

FOOL                     I took this lid,
And all the women screamed at me.
I took the spit, and all screamed worse.
A shoulder of lamb stood ready for the roasting—

---

like the Blind Man also from *On Baile's Strand* who cuts the hero's throat in *The Death of Cuchulain* (1939), Yeats's last play.

    91. "a large stone" Congal's men stoned the herne; with characteristic irony the herne arranges for stones to secure the spit for Congal's death.

    92. "Widow Rooney's kitchen" The Fool's account of the start of his "quest" recalls early Abbey Theatre plays like *The Pot of Broth* (1904) or the comedies of Lady Gregory, Synge, and George Fitzmaurice.

I put the pot upon my head.
They did not scream but stood and gaped.

[*Fool arms himself with spit, cauldron lid and pot, whistling 'The Great Herne's Feather'.*]⁹³

CONGAL   But⁹⁴ why must you kill Congal, Fool?
What harm has he done you?

FOOL                              None at all.
But there's a Fool called Johnny from Meath,⁹⁵
We are great rivals and we hate each other,
But I can get the pennies if I kill Congal,
And Johnny nothing.

CONGAL                    I am King Congal,
And is not that a thing to laugh at, Fool?

FOOL   Very nice, O very nice indeed,
For I can kill you now, and I
Am tired of walking.

CONGAL                      Both need rest.
Another drink apiece—that is done—
Lead to the place you have cleared of stones.

FOOL   But where is your sword? You have not got a sword.

CONGAL   I lost it, or I never had it,
Or threw it at the strange donkey below,⁹⁶
But that's no matter—I have hands.

[*They go out at one side. Attracta, Corney and Donkey come in. Attracta sings.*]

---

93. "whistling 'The Great Herne's Feather'" Aligns Fool with the herne god and motivates Attracta's entry later. *1952* adds "Hush, that is an unlucky tune!"

94. "But" *1952*: "And"

95. "Meath" One of the Fifths of Ireland, it now includes County Meath and is the area in which Tara is situated.

96. "Or threw it at the strange donkey below" Congal is referring to his sword and to his soul, in Yeats's symbolism (cf. Sato's Sword in "A Dialogue of Self and Soul"); unwittingly he describes the punishment reserved for him, and which no one yet knows: his soul will fly from his dying body to lodge in a newly conceived donkey.

# SCENE VI

ATTRACTA   When beak and claw their work began[97]
What horror stirred in the roots of my hair?
*Sang the bride of the Herne, and the Great Herne's bride.*
But who lay there in the cold dawn,
When all that terror had come and gone?
Was I the woman lying there?

[*They go out. Congal and Tom the Fool come. Congal is carrying the cauldron lid, pot and spit. He lays them down.*]

CONGAL   I was sent to die at the hands of a Fool.
There must be another Fool on the mountain.

FOOL   That must be Johnny from Meath.
But that's a thing I could not endure,
For Johnny would get all the pennies.

CONGAL   Here, take a drink and have no fear;
All's plain at last; though I shall die
I shall not die at a Fool's hand.
I have thought out a better plan.
I and the Herne have had three bouts,[98]
He won the first, I won the second,
Six men and I possessed his wife.

FOOL   I ran after a woman once.
I had seen two donkeys in a field.

CONGAL   And did you get her, did you get her, Fool?

FOOL   I almost had my hand upon her.
She screamed, and somebody came and beat me.
Were you beaten?

---

97. "When beak and claw their work began" The second half of the marriage song, or epithalamium, describes the weapons a bird uses to kill; hence it becomes both wedding song and funeral dirge, appropriate in one who is both womb and funeral urn.

98. "I and the Herne have had three bouts" Jeffares notes, "The first was the fall into disorder and the death of Aedh; the second the rape of Attracta" (*Com. Pl.*, 272, n. 693). The third, to be won by the herne, starts with the thunder scene and ends with Congal's transmigration into a donkey.

CONGAL          No, no, Fool.
          But she said that nobody had touched her,
          And after that the thunder said the same,
          Yet I had won that bout, and now
          I know that I shall win the third.

FOOL      If Johnny from Meath comes, kill him!

CONGAL    Maybe I will, maybe I will not.

FOOL      You let me off, but don't let him off.

CONGAL    I could not do you any harm,
          For you and I are friends.

FOOL                      Kill Johnny!

CONGAL    Because you have asked me to, I will do it,
          For you and I are friends.

FOOL                      Kill Johnny!
          Kill with the spear, but give it to me
          That I may see if it is sharp enough.

[*Fool takes spit.*]

CONGAL    And is it, Fool?

FOOL                      I spent an hour
          Sharpening it upon a stone.
          Could I kill you now?

CONGAL                    Maybe you could.

FOOL      I will get all the pennies for myself.

[*He wounds Congal. The wounding is symbolised by a movement of the spit towards or over Congal's body.*]

CONGAL    It passed out of your mind for a moment
          That we are friends, but that is natural.

## SCENE VI

FOOL
*[dropping spit]*
I must see it, I never saw a wound.

CONGAL  The Herne has got the first blow in;[99]
A scratch, a scratch, a mere nothing.
But had it been a little deeper and higher
It would have gone through the heart, and maybe
That would have left me better off,
For the Great Herne may beat me in the end.
Here I must sit through the full moon,
And he will send up Fools against me,
Meandering, roaring, yelling,
Whispering Fools, then chattering Fools,
And after that morose, melancholy,
Sluggish, fat, silent Fools;
And I, moon-crazed, moon-blind,[100]
Fighting and wounded, wounded and fighting.
I never thought of such an end.
Never be a soldier, Tom;
Though it begins well, is this a life?
If this is a man's life, is there any life
But a dog's life?[101]

FOOL  That's it, that's it;
Many a time they have put a dog at me.

CONGAL  If I should give myself a wound,
Let life run away, I'd win the bout.
He said I must die at the hands of a Fool
And sent you hither. Give me that spit!
I put it in this crevice of the rock,

---

99. "The Herne has got the first blow in" A wound in the rib cage, to judge by the next sentence. A parody of heroic combat, and perhaps the wounding of Christ by a spear, though the spit is long and sharp like a heron's beak.

100. "And I, moon-crazed, moon blind" Congal is an objective (sun) type living under a subjective (moon) god, the herne, and thus not in phase with his cycle. That is why he fights the herne, and why he is defeated.

101. "a dog's life" Congal's meditation on the soldier's life followed by the thought of a dog is a concise reprise of scene 1.

That I may fall upon the point.
These stones will keep it sticking upright.
[*They arrange stones, he puts the spit in.*]

CONGAL

[*almost screaming in his excitement*]
    Fool! Am I myself a Fool?
    For if I am a Fool, he wins the bout.

FOOL    You are King of Connaught. If you were a fool
    They would have chased you with their dogs.

CONGAL    I am King Congal of Connaught and of Tara,
    That wise, victorious, voluble, unlucky,
    Blasphemous, famous, infamous man.
    Fool, take this spit when red with blood,
    Show it to the people and get all the pennies;
    What does it matter what they think?
    The Great Herne knows that I have won.

[*He falls symbolically upon the spit. It does not touch him. Fool takes the spit and wine-skin and goes out.*]
    It seems that I am hard to kill,
    But the wound is deep. Are you up there?
    Your chosen kitchen spit has killed me,
    But killed me at my own will, not yours.

[*Attracta and Corney enter. The moon rises.*][102]

ATTRACTA    Will the knot hold?

CORNEY    There was a look
    About the old highwayman's eye of him
    That warned me, so I made him fast
    To that old stump among the rocks
    With a great knot that he can neither
    Break, nor pull apart with his teeth.

---

102. "enter. The moon rises" *1952*: "enter."

## SCENE VI

CONGAL   Attracta!

ATTRACTA   I called you to this place,[103]
You came, and now the story is finished.

CONGAL   You have great powers, even the thunder
Does whatever you bid it do.[104]
Protect me, I have won my bout,
But I am afraid of what the Herne
May do with me when I am dead.
I am afraid that he may put me
Into the shape of a brute beast.

ATTRACTA   I will protect you if, as I think,
Your shape is not yet fixed upon.

CONGAL   I am slipping now, and you up there[105]
With your long leg and your long beak.
But I have beaten you, Great Herne,
In spite of your kitchen spit—seven men—

*[He dies.]*

ATTRACTA   Come lie with me upon the ground,
Come quickly into my arms, come quickly, come
Before his body has had time to cool.

CORNEY   What? Lie with you?

ATTRACTA   Lie and beget.[106]
If you are afraid of the Great Herne,

---

103. "I called you to this place," Though Congal thinks he has won the third bout, he can be seen as merely an actor in the god's story, from whose standpoint Congal dies at the hands of a fool (himself), thus hurrying to the punishment he fears, rebirth as an animal.

104. "bid it do." *Variorum*: "bid it to do." No authority given.

105. "I am slipping now, and you up there" Possibly a use of Irish syntax to mean that as Congal slips toward death, he acknowledges the herne's presence above him. Common English idiom could mean that both Congal and herne are slipping, a reading that fits with the play as dramatizing a change of god, from the subjective herne to the objective Christ.

106. "beget." as *1952 1938*: "beget,"

                    Put that away, for if I do his will,
                    You are his instrument or himself.

CORNEY              The thunder has me terrified.

ATTRACTA            I lay with the Great Herne, and he,
                    Being all a spirit, but begot
                    His image in the mirror of my spirit,[107]
                    Being all sufficient to himself
                    Begot himself; but there's a work
                    That should be done, and that work needs[108]
                    The imperfection of a man.

[*The sound of a donkey braying.*][109]

CORNEY              The donkey is braying.
                    He has some wickedness in his mind.

ATTRACTA            Too late, too late, he broke that knot,
                    And there, down there among the rocks
                    He couples with another donkey.
                    That donkey has conceived, I thought that I
                    Could give a human form to Congal,
                    But now he must be born a donkey.

CORNEY              King Congal must be born a donkey!

ATTRACTA            Because we were not quick enough.

CORNEY              I have heard that a donkey carries its young
                    Longer than any other beast,
                    Thirteen months it must carry it.

---

107. "but begot . . . my spirit," Wholly spirit, the god left only its spirit's image reflected in Attracta's soul. To beget another human being, in which Congal's soul may be reborn, Attracta needs to couple with imperfect man, i.e., Corney. Her insight is that of *A Full Moon in March*: "What can she lack whose emblem is the moon? / But desecration and the lover's night."

108. "needs" *1952* adds "No bird's beak nor claw, but a man,"

109. "The sound of a donkey braying" In *The Player Queen* this sound heralds the end of a cycle. Here the end of the cycle and the punishment of Congal's soul coincide; both Congal and the herne have lost this bout.

## SCENE VI

[*He laughs.*]
All that trouble and nothing to show for it,
Nothing but just another donkey.


THE END